Laughton Osborn

The Magnetiser The Prodigal

Comedies in Prose

Laughton Osborn

The Magnetiser The Prodigal
Comedies in Prose

ISBN/EAN: 9783744784160

Printed in Europe, USA, Canada, Australia, Japan

Cover: Foto ©Andreas Hilbeck / pixelio.de

More available books at **www.hansebooks.com**

THE MAGNETISER

THE PRODIGAL

COMEDIES IN PROSE

BY

LAUGHTON OSBORN

NEW YORK
JAMES MILLER, 647 BROADWAY
MDCCCLXIX

THE MAGNETISER

OR

READY FOR ANYBODY

MDCCCXLII

CHARACTERS

CLAIRVOIR,   *a wealthy widower.*

RACY,   *his half-brother.*

SCHUYLER WALTON,   *engaged to Clairvoir's daughter.*

FRANK RANDOLPH,   *a young Virginian, nephew to Racy through his wife, and his son and heir by adoption.*

ARNOLD DULRUSE,   *engaged to Clairvoir's niece.*

SANZACARLINI,   *a needy Neapolitan.*

GANTELET,   *French servant to Randolph.*

CATHARINE,   *Clairvoir's daughter.*

MARY MILDMAY,   *his niece.*

MRS. DULRUSE,   *his housekeeper, — Arnold's mother.*

LETTY,   *Catharine's maid.*

SCENE.   *New York.*

TIME.   *That occupied by the action.*

THE MAGNETISER

ACT THE FIRST

SCENE I. *In Clairvoir's house. — A drawingroom, with three windows, having Venetian blinds on the outside. The sashes of the windows are raised, and the blinds of one of them bowed, with the laths inclining downward. At this latter window, MARY MILDMAY is seen sitting, in a listless attitude, as though she was looking idly into the street; her cheek rests upon one hand, while the other holds some needlework negligently upon her lap.*

Enter
CATHARINE, *gaily. She runs up to* MARY, *clapping her hands together.*

Cath. They 're at it! they 're at it! Coz! cousin Mary! Why, what the deuse is in the girl? [*shaking her.*] Here is the greatest sport in the world going on, and all within doors; yet you sit there moping, gazing through the blinds at ash-carts and omnibuses, as if there was poetry in dust and music in wagon-wheels. ¹Come along, there 's a dear! Have you no respect for science? no regard [*pompously.*] for the exaltation of human nature by the demonstration of magnetical affinities? ha, ha, ha!

Mary. I am not in spirits, Kate.

Cath. [*Mimicking.*] Not in spirits, Kate! Not in liquor, I suppose. Now, if you were a man, I should verily believe you were. But I 'll tell you what you are in, Mary; you 're in love; and that 's the most spiritless thing in the world, I 'm sure.

Mary. [*Rising.*] I should hope not, cousin; for then, poor Mr. Walton!

Cath. Well, that sounds somewhat like life. And now, since you are fairly roused, let us off to the library. [*Brings her forward.*] Come, instead of watching for Mr. Arnold Dulruse, let us see what Mr. Arnold's mother is doing to my papa and your uncle.

Mary. But, Kate dear, how can you tease one so? You know I never — that is — I mean — I never now like to talk of Arnold.

Cath. No, but — that is — I mean — you love to think on him. Ha, ha! my gentle, and most constant, and grave, and pensive Mary, how you blush!

Mary. You have bad eyes, cousin.

Cath. Then Schuyler tells me very great fibs. The dear, good-for-nothing, rhyming! —— Did n't he say, that — Let me see, what was it? — O! [*Declaiming.*] "Oh, by those eyes, whose rays are like" — are like — O! "are like the stars, That through the blue of heaven their" —— and so on. There! you malicious little devil, you see that I am greater than Atlas; I bear a firmament between my eyelids, and am a sort of peripatetic animated universe, or at least a circumambulatory supercelestial! Bad eyes, you envious creature? Stars! stars! and of the first magnitude. When did your dull prosaic lover ever say anything half so fine to you?

Mary. Why, in truth, never. And I am much obliged to him; for, had he likened my eyes to stars, I should have thought that he felt himself in the dark when under their beams, and that a release to the streets was a welcome escape into daylight, or a waking from the night into morning. Of trite similes, the sun is rather more cheerful and vivifying, if one must have such celestial nonsense.

Cath. I vow, I'll pinch you to death. But come, coz.

Mary. Where?

Cath. To see papa play blindman's-buff with Mrs. Dulruse in the library. ²Letty saw them go there a minute ago. By this time, the curtain must be up, and the farce will want spectators. Come, Mary darling, I wouldn't miss the scene for worlds.

Mary. But cannot you go alone, Kate? I would rather — I would rather not go; because — because ——

Cath. Because you would rather stay here, to look from the window, and fancy that every orangeman you see is about to be metamorphosed into sober Mr. Dulruse, with his arm full of golden compliments and fragrant suavities, just imported from Cyprus, and to wish that the next image-vender were your solemn beau, with all his little plaster Cupids turned into spiritual, ardent, real Loves, and nestling in his head, instead of spreading their squab wings on the boarded top of it.

Mary. Indeed, indeed, Catharine, you mistake me : I was not — not looking for Arnold. [*Bursts into tears.*

Cath. [*Kissing and embracing her affectionately.*] And suppose that you were, dear, good Mary ! Now, do forgive me : indeed, indeed I did not mean to vex you ; and I cannot see any harm in one's wishing for one's sweetheart. There ! kiss, to show that you forgive me.

Mary. But there is no harm done, Kate ; and I am not angry.

Cath. No, you dear soul, you are too sweet-tempered ever for that. [*Kissing her again and embracing.*

Mary. Come, cousin ; don't mistake me for yourself, and yourself for Mr. Walton.

Cath. Not quite, or you would not have had that kiss.

Mary. Hum !

Cath. Now, I *will* pinch you. You 're a naughty, malicious ——

Mary. Oh yes ! an old receipt to hide confusion. Whose turn is it now, Kate ? [*Ringing within.*] Ah !

Cath. Why, yours again ; and to lose color, too. I told you, you expected ——

Mary. No, Kate upon my word ! Indeed ! I am sure it is *not* he. That is Mr. Walton.

Cath. A dozen pairs of gloves, it is not ! Run to the window ; you can't be seen. Psha ! you 're a snail ! Let me. [*Looks through the blinds for a second, and comes back blushing and confused.*

Mary. You 've lost ! I knew it. And you never lost a wager more willingly.

Cath. Not since it gives you pain, believe me, dear Mary. But where is the girl going? Mr. Walton wont eat you up.

Mary. No, but he would be cross enough to snap at me, if I staid. There 's the door shut! Three spoils company. [*Going.*

Cath. And one should do, as one would be done by, ah, coz! [*Running after and hugging her. Exit Mary.*] The dear, sweet girl! What a pity she should have such a lover!

Enter WALTON.

Walt. What lover is that, Catharine, that is so happy as to be the object of your pity?

Cath. Not you, Schuyler; or I should wish you far enough.

Walt. Why, yes; for Pity, if akin to Love, is one of that sort of poor relations we are seldom proud to acknowledge.

Cath. True; for, nine times out of ten, Contempt is in the family.

Walt. And the tenth time, she may be found to be a twin-sister. Happy fellow! if such is the lineage of the gentleman in question.

Cath. Why, whom are you talking of now?

Walt. The lover, surely, whom you named as I entered.

Cath. It would fit him well, in that case. But my pity was not bestowed upon the lover, but the lady. Poor Mary!

Walt. Your cousin, Miss Mildmay?

Cath. Yes; and I wonder more and more, every day, what a girl of her good taste could have seen in that sour Mr.

Dulruse to bewitch her. [3] He is quite unworthy of so good a girl, I am sure; and some other man might one day make her far happier, than her tender nature could ever hope to be with a person of his character.

Walt. Generous creature! I do love you so, for that very love you bear your orphan cousin!

Cath. What! more than for my eyes? the *stars*, you know. Take care, Mr. Poet; I shall be jealous.

Walt. And you will have cause, Catharine, whenever your virtues shall seem inferior to Miss Mildmay's.

Cath. And are my eyes then to count for nothing? O sacrilegious and rebellious subject! I must have you to your rhymes again. When did I give you leave to forget my beauty in the catalogue of my numerous qualifications?

Walt. When you taught me that your heart outshone it, and that your mind was its divinest essence. [*Kissing her hand.*

Cath. Well, pretty well, that: your disloyalty is atoned for. And now, let go my fingers, and I will tell you a secret. First, what do you think of Mrs. Dulruse?

Walt. If my position will excuse my speaking so plainly —— Yet, I would rather not.

[4] *Cath.* Fy! what scrupulosity! Why, she is but our housekeeper — as yet, thank Heaven! — and you know I do not like her.

Walt. Yet, she is a lady, — at least, she has been so accounted; and, at all events, she is a woman.

Cath. Well then, since you are so delicate, I will be your mouthpiece. [5] I will speak for you; and you shall see how well I can read your thought.

Walt. Take care you don't misspell.

Cath. You shall ferule my hand, if I do. Nay, don't take hold of it, already; I have not yet missed. — You think her, Schuyler, an artful, heartless, and mercenary woman, whose will, were it but assisted by her intellect, would render her dangerous; but her ignorance makes her blunder, and her scheming degenerates, through her fatuity, into mere cunning.

Walt. Which is the intelligence of vulgar minds. You have read me well. Now, what follows?

Cath. How would you like her for a mother-in-law?

Walt. Like her? But that is impossible!

Cath. Indeed! What then, if she become my mother?

Walt. Good Heaven! your father — Mr. Clairvoir cannot be so blind?

Cath. Indeed, but he is: the deluded are always so. And they are this very moment about it.

Walt. Surely, it cannot be; there is some mistake; you are not so unhappy. Gone to be married!

Cath. I did not say so. But they are going through the preliminaries; courtship and infatuation.

Walt. I do not understand you. You talk, Catharine, of what should be a misery to you, yet there is a lurking humor in those darling eyes, and a smile about those beautiful lips, that ——

Cath. I had better tell you at once, I see; for you are lapsing into poetry and flattery. — Did you ever hear of Animal Magnetism, or Mesmerism, or whatever other *ism*, except skepticism, you may choose to name it.

Walt. Surely. Who has not?

Cath. And do you believe in it?

Walt. Do I believe that I can see without eyes, hear without ears, smell without a nose, taste without a tongue, and feel without either feet or hands?

Cath. Well, my father does; and some books that he has lately been reading have carried his credulity to a pitch that is absolute fanaticism. Now, Mrs. Dulruse has for a long time been making love to him.

Walt. Nothing uncommon in the housekeeper of a wealthy widower.

Cath. So I suppose; but it is not the more agreeable for all that. Well, what does the cunning creature do, but gradually, after a little well-managed resistance, become a convert to these fantastical doctrines. My father, of course, was vastly delighted; [6] the more so that I had made free to ridicule their nonsense; and conceiving there might be some undiscovered magnetic affinities between himself and the amiable Dulruse, he yesterday set himself to explore the localities, doubtless with the full consent of the proprietress. My Letty took the liberty of listening and peeping at the keyhole of the library, [7] where the experiments were performed. I have reprimanded her: but I could not prevent myself from hearing what she came in all haste to tell me. You look grave, Schuyler. Was I wrong?

Walt. I think you were; you should have stopped her at once, my dear girl.

Cath. And I believe I should; but Letty took me quite by surprise, and, before I knew what I was about, had emptied her budget for my benefit. And what do you think it amounted to?

Walt. I do not like to guess.

Cath. Why, that Mrs. Dulruse has a design to entrap my father into a speedy, if not immediate marriage.

Walt. But the girl may have deceived herself.

Cath. No, no; she is the cleverest maid ever lady was blest with.   [8] Besides, my dear Schuyler, I drew the same conclusion from what she told me, as she herself had done.   Now, have you a desire to observe this folly?

Walt. How?

Cath. Just before you came in, papa led his innamorata to the library, Letty tells me; and there is no doubt he is now manipulating on her wrinkled sinciput, and making, as he supposes, (I should blush to say it of my father to anybody but you,) his spirit pass into hers over the very ethereal bridge of his thumbs.   I wanted Mary to go in with me; but she refused, poor thing, I suspect, because of late — from — from — for a certain reason I cannot name to you now, Mrs. Dulruse has treated her with no little insolence.

Walt. But how will your father relish our intrusion?

Cath. Be delighted with it.   He will glory in the demonstration of his fancied science.   Come.   [9] But first, we'll endeavor to persuade Mary to join us.   I long to open her eyes to the character of the Dulruses, mother and son.   She should not marry that man.

Walt. You are very right: she were better dead.   I will go with you.

Cath. Mary is in the next room.   Before we go to the library, Letty shall repeat to you all she knows of this intrigue, as I fear it to be on one side.   Do not hesitate; the girl is not

2*

an ordinary servant.   And besides, Schuyler, nothing, that is not dishonorable, should stand in our way, to prevent a consummation as melancholy almost for you as it would be for me.

Walt. Sensible girl! [*Kissing her hand.*

Cath. Fy! you are as bad as my father.   Does good sense lie in the fingers ?

Walt. No, Kate, but a most delicate sensation does. [*Exeunt, at the side.*

Scene II.

A room of smaller dimensions, surrounded with shelves of books. Globes, maps, and the various other articles usual in a private library. — Mrs. Dulruse is discovered seated in a high-backed arm-chair, in the position and with the appearance proper to the magnetic slumber. Clairvoir seated before her in another chair.   Just as the scene opens, he throws himself back in his seat, and gazes with a show of admiration on his patient.

Clair. Wonderful, celestial science !   [10] Where now are the primordial bounds which would-be philosophers have pretended were set by Nature to human action and to human thought ?   [11] Man, no longer a creature of the elements, no more a slave to the narrow powers exerted by mere blood, and bones, and muscle, man, the spirit not the carcase, shall not

say unto the worm, " Thou art my mother and my sister ",
but unto the angels, Ye are my brethren: for he is, now, all-
seeing, ubiquitous, — ah! he may be omniscient. Not now
he needs to pass at peril of his life to foreign countries.
Seated in his chair, he wills himself into the mind of another
and congenial spirit, who, at his direction travels in thought
to all quarters of the world, without moving an inch,—[12] sees
now the British massacre in China, now counts the Arabs
slaughtered at Algiers, now prognosticates the sex of the
forthcoming issue of Victoria; and the tardy conveyance and
uncertain news, of mails and steamboats, are entirely superseded. Hail mysterious source —— What am I doing? I,
who till now have ridiculed soliloquies, am in my rapture
guilty of that folly! Yet no; I do not speak alone and to
myself; there sits my coadjutor, my sympathetic Dolly; and
doubtless, at this moment, though locked, by the semi-gyra-
tion of my thumbs in a slumber which a park of artillery
could not disturb, she hears all, and sees all, as though she
was awake. Do you not, madam?

Mrs. D. As clear as starch.

Clair. I thought so! I thought so! Wonderful! — A few
more experiments, and I will release you from this fatiguing,
though ecstatic trance. Let us mount into the moon: I want
to know what the people there are doing. Here, give me
your hands.

Mrs. D. But you must n't let me fall.

Clair. Never fear, madam. Are you ready? Let us fly
then? [*He lifts her hands up and down, to imitate the motion of
wings.*

Mrs. D. O, what a wondersome height! But I shall fall! Mercy on me! my head goes round like a top.

Clair. Hold fast then. And, faith, you do! you squeeze like the devil. Not quite so hard. There; are you there?

Mrs. D. Yes, I am in a wonderful place. It does n't look at all like green cheese: that must be a fib.

Clair. No doubt; no doubt. Do you see any mountains, madam, and valleys?

Mrs. D. Yes, a great many of 'em; one ever so high! six times as high as the Katskills — and with trees growing on the top of it. Lor'! it 's shaped like a man's nose! It must be part of the face we see in the full moon.

Clair. Very likely. But they must have a peculiar climate there, for trees to grow at such a height.

Mrs. D. Yes; but then, there are none in the valleys.

Clair. Ah! I see! I see. That explains it. Everything is just the reverse of what it is here on earth. Wonderful!

Mrs. D. O yes; there goes a man, walking as fast as ever he can, on his head. Good gracious!

Clair. Are you sure?

Mrs. D. Yes; for he meets a lady, and they touch heels together.

Clair. Toes, you mean.

Mrs. D. Yes, toes, to salute one another.

Clair. How are they dressed?

Mrs. D. Spare my blushes. I do declare — I —— Don't ask me; but I don't think they have anything on them; not a rag. The indecent creatures!

Clair. A state of innocence and unsophisticated nature.

No stocks there fluctuate with the rise and fall of cotton; no quarrels threaten from an agitated tariff on silks.[13] Do you see any water?

Mrs. D. Oceans full; and, my stars! there is a man on the shore, milking a whale! Did you ever?

Clair. The very thing the moon-hoax said! I never could have believed it. Does he do it standing?

Mrs. D. No, he 's lying on his face, feet foremost.

Clair. And draws the udder with his toes! A strange variety of the genus *Homo.*[14] Are you tired, my dear? Shall we descend?

Mrs. D. If you please; it feels so cold here. [*she shudders and makes her teeth chatter.*] But don't let me fall.

Clair. Never fear. [*She puts her arm about his neck.*] That 's right. But, the deuse! don't hug so hard; or you'll strangle me. There! are you home?

Mrs. D. Yes. O me! I 'm so tired!

Clair. And what do you see here?

Mrs. D. Mr. Walton 's in the drawingroom, courting Miss Clairvoir.

Clair. Like enough; the bell rung a little while ago. Well, that is all right.

Mrs. D. Ah, I 'm afeard not!

Clair. No? Why not?

Mrs. D. She never will marry him.

Clair. The deuse she wont! This is bad news. Are you very sure?

Mrs. D. Yes, another match is laid out for her, that will make her ever so much happier. He will be the richest

man in town, twice as rich as John Jacob [15] Astor; and they
will have lots of children.

Clair. But who is he? who is he?

Mrs. D. I blush to say.   [16] Do not ask me.

Clair. Nay, dear madam, speak out; nobody hears you.

Mrs. D. But will you forgive me?

Clair. Surely; I cannot help fate; you see but what will
happen.

Mrs. D. And what ought to happen; for shockin' things
'll take place if it don't.   It is ——

Clair. Who?

Mrs. D. His name begins with A, and ends with E.

Clair. A? And ends with E? Who can that be? [*to
himself.*

Mrs. D. Now I see him clearly.   What a handsome young
man! He kneels to ask my blessing; and his wife kneels to
ask her father's.   What a lovely couple! It is my son! my
Arnold! Did I ever!

Clair. Why no, I never! This I don't like.

Mrs. D. But it's writ in Heaven, and must be.

Clair. But perhaps we may avoid it; for I tell you, widow,
she is promised to Schuyler Walton, as fine a fellow as ever
darkened a house-door: — and there are other reasons
besides.

Mrs. D. But what must be will be; and Mr. Walton laughs
at the science, and mocks at you.

Clair. How do you know that? Did you ever hear him?

Mrs. D. No, but I see it as plain as I see the whales, and
everything in this sumnamberlism.

Clair. Somnambulism, my dear. If I thought so —— But what else do you see? What is my dearest wish at this moment? Come, tell me that; it is my last experiment for to-day.

Mrs. D. It is —— Spare my blushes.

Clair. Pshaw! my dear; no one sees you, but me.

Mrs. D. That's true. And then I'm forced to speak; or I would n't. Your dearest wish is —

Clair. To? —

Mrs. D. Consermate our union. [*Clairvoir starts back, and Mrs. D. covers her face as if ashamed.*

Clair. The devil it is! Why, I never thought of it! Are you very sure, Mrs. Dulruse?

Mrs. D. Posertive, Mr. Clairvoir.

Clair. Then I don't know my own mind.

Mrs. D. How should you as well as I? Did n't you give me the power to enter it? I can't help it, if you willed it so. And you might have a thought, you know, which was kind o' dim to yourself, but which I could see ever so plain.

Clair. And that is true; for you are fast asleep.

Mrs. D. Besides, what was you just talking of? Wasn't it of Mr. Walton and Miss Catharine?

Clair. True.

Mrs. D. Well, what so near to a father as his daughter? So, thinking of her, you must have thought of yourself, you know, and, thinking of her marriage, your own must have occurred to you, don't you see, and, having occurred to you, why, you must have wished it at this moment.

Clair. Why, that I am not so sure of. But in all the rest

you reason like a philosopher; and the science cannot be mistaken.

Mrs. D. Nor can I resist your will, Mr. Clairvoir. If you was to send me to the Bad Place, I must go there; and if you willed me to look into your mind, I had to do it: your power is omipertent.

Clair. Angelic creature! [*Throws his arm in ecstacy about her neck.*] What a union of congenial spirits will ours be!

Mrs. D. Yes, what a union of convenience! Dear Mr. Clairvoir! [*throwing her arms in turn about him.*] Oh, dear me! I shall die of shame!

Clair. Poor soul! She cannot help betraying her love in this magnetic condition!

Mrs. D. No, in this pathetic position I cannot indeed help displaying it. [*kisses him.*

Enter

WALTON *and* CATHARINE,

who stop, confused, and gaze at one another.

Clair. What a life of immateriality will ours be!

Mrs. D. Yes, pure materiality! [*kissing him.*

Clair. No corporeity to obfuscate our intellectual enjoyments.

Mrs. D. No, no paupereity to fuzzball our effectual enjoyments! Oh, my love! [*hugging him.*

Clair. We shall see with magnetic vision, feel by magnetic affinity, [17] get our children by magnetic conjunction ——

Mrs. D. O, Mr. Clairvoir! spare my blushes!

Clair. — Do all things by magnetic, somnambulistic, sympathetic correspondence. A life of unsensuality, without admixture! [*hugging.*

Mrs. D. Yes, a life of sensuality, without fixtures! Let us begin it at once. O, O, O, dear, darling, apathetic magnetiser! [*hugging.*

Cath. [*recovering. Aside to Walton.*] What say you now? O my father! Let us go.

Walt. [*aside to Cath.*] Right. A child should never be the willing observer of a parent's follies.

Clair. [*standing up and disengaging himself.*] Eh! what's that? Confusion!

Mrs. D. [*pretending to be still fast asleep.*] Clairvoir, don't leave me.

Clair. Hush, Mrs. D.! there are persons present. Poor thing! she can see and hear only me. Wonderful! — Mr. Walton — Catharine — don't go. Mrs. Dulruse has been so kind as to permit me to manipulate her. I have made some wonderful experiments. Would you like to see them continued?

Cath. No, no, papa; we will go. Come; [*aside to Walton.*] don't stay.

Clair. But Mr. Walton [*detaining Walt.*] would perhaps like to see them, Kate. And my wish was, just this moment, (at least, I thought so; though Mrs. Dulruse says it was not,) to have spectators of my great discoveries. Come, Walton, my boy; I will put her into communication with you. Take her hand.

Mrs. D. O no, Mr. Clairvoir, don't! I don't want to have [18] evil communication with anybody but you.

Walt. You had better wake her up, sir,— if she is not so already.

Clair. So already! Walton! Schuyler Walton! Are you stupid? Why, sir — look at that excellent woman. Not a park of artillery exploding in her ears would wake her; not the thunder of heaven, sir; yet I, I, sir, poor human being as I am, I, Harry Clairvoir, can rouse her by the will, by the mere energy of my spirit! Behold!

Cath. O dear! my father is stark mad. [*aside.*

Clair. Awake, Mrs. Dulruse! awake to this grosser existence! [*waving his hand magnetically over her forehead.*] I will it.

Mrs. D. [*starting and opening her eyes.*] Where? — What's the matter? [*Rubbing her eyes, and staring round in seeming confusion.*] Who? — O! I see! I am dead with shame.

Clair. You should be alive with glory, Mrs. Dulruse! [*Taking her hand.*] It is the victory of science; the triumph of immortal mind over corrupt matter; the exaltation of spirituality over corporality! Walton, study magnetism; I will lend you [19] Townshend, Hartshorne, all of them; your sons shall be magnetisers, and your daughters ——

Walt. [*aside to Cath.*] Dulruses, I suppose. — I thank you, sir; I am quite contented that they should have their simple senses like their father, and their every-day virtues like their lovely mother. [*Exeunt Walt. and Cath.*

Clair. Sir! no respect for your immortal nature? no belief in the mind's independence of the corporeal faculties? [*Turning before Walt. and Cath. are quite gone.*] Did you ever, Mrs. Dulruse?

Mrs. D. Why no, I never! And I must say, Mr. Clair-voir —

Clair. That Walton treats me most shabbily. Look you, sir! Eh! gone? In my own house? [20] *He*, I see plainly, has no sympathy with science, no congeniality of feeling.

Mrs. D. I told you so: no conveniality for feeling at all.

Clair. But I'll settle him!

Mrs. D. You'd best let Miss Catharine.

Clair. Perhaps I may. The disrespectful! —— Simple senses, indeed! The sense for simply stale precedents. Mere corporality; no ethereality of sentiment; no power of pro-spective ratiocination! Come, my better half.

Mrs. D. [*affecting coyness.*] I am not so yet, sir.

Clair. Yes, in your spirit.

Mrs. D. But my body? —

Clair. I'll magnetise that to-morrow. [*Going.*

Mrs. D. But the ring will be well to keep it fast, Mr. Clair-voir. [*Lagging behind.*

Clair, Time enough for that, [21] my congenial spirit. — Mere corporality! no ethereality! no reverence for this mystic agent! [*Exit, shutting the door after him in his abstraction.*

Mrs. D. Time enough, you old fool, you? Let me get it once, and I'll make my body fast enough to you. That [*snapping her fingers.*] for your Geneva spirits and queer realities! that for your pauperalities and Fiscal Agents! [*Exit.*

ACT THE SECOND

SCENE I. *The Drawingroom, as in Act I. Sc. I. — Enter*
CATHARINE, *followed by* DULRUSE.

Cath. You carry your presumption, sir, rather too far for a
gentleman. Or, are you so dull that you cannot take a hint?

Dulr. So devoted that I will not take it. You have left the
other room, Miss Clairvoir, to avoid me; and I have followed,
because I will not be avoided.

Cath. Sir! sir!

Dulr. I say so, Miss Catharine. Love is not so easily re-
pulsed.

Cath. This is too insolent! Leave me, this instant: and,
for your odious pretensions —

Dulr. But —

Cath. — Odious pretensions, — if you dare repeat them,
my father shall forbid you the house. Go, sir.

Dulr. Madam, I cannot see what you mean by *odious*. If a
sincere, and respectful adoration —

Cath. — Of fifty thousand dollars and large expectations ——

Dulr. You mistake, you mistake. It is yourself, your be-
witching person, your exalted character, that I adore; money
is no consideration, where —

Cath. — It is so inconsiderable as with Miss Mildmay.

Her poor ten thousand are quite beneath the regards of an aspirer like Mr. Arnold Dulruse.

Dulr. [*muttered and aside.*] D—nation! [22]

Cath. You might as well swear louder, Mr. Dulruse. If you are ashamed that your meanness is detected, go and repent it.

Dulr. Miss Clairvoir, do not be so hasty! Hear me. I did indeed once love your cousin —

Cath. Oh sir!

Dulr. — But was it possible, when you were present —

Cath. — To adore her longer? No! [*Affecting pompousness.*] Who sees the stars when the moon is in her glory? and when the golden sun arises in the orient, is not her silver round unnoticed in the west? Is that the style, sir? *Gold* and *silver*, you see: a great difference. There; you now perceive that you are laughed at, and you turn pale with rage. To be serious: have you forgotten that there is a person in the world by the name of Walton?

Dulr. But my mother —

Cath. Your mother?

Dulr. Don't speak so scornfully, Miss Clairvoir; that mother may be yours before long; yes, will be. Who is pale, now? Come, Miss Catharine, let us talk reason. I have not only my mother's assurance —

Cath. — But also your own; which is fully equal.

Dulr. — But also your father approves of my passion. You may look incredulous. And what is more, he has not only taken me into favor, but Mr. Walton, he declares, shall never have you.

Cath. It is false; false as your pretended passion. I shall ask him this instant. [*As she is going to the door, Dulruse puts himself in the way.*] Stand out of my way, sir.

Dulr. But hear me.

Cath. Let me pass, this instant, as you value your safety. I have been, I see, too backward, too forbearing. I wished to spare Miss Mildmay's feelings, and I was silent; I did not care to involve Mr. Walton in a quarrel, and I forbore to tell him; and, for the sake of all concerned, I have withheld your preposterous and insulting declarations from Mr. Clairvoir: but, since this is misunderstood, my patience is at an end; and the next word that you dare address me on this subject, you shall hear your answer from one that will make more impression on you. Let me pass, sir. [*Exit.*

Dulr. [*between his teeth.*] And the devil go with you, for a pert, insolent, purse-proud! —— Death and furies! [*Exit.*

Scene II.

The Dining-room at Mr. Clairvoir's. *Enter* Letty, *looking for something.*

Letty. [*singing.*

" Still so gently o'er me stealing,
Memory will bring back the feeling " ——

Enter DULRUSE.

*He starts, looks pleased, then goes behind her
cautiously, and, as she concludes the second verse, puts his hand
about her waist.*

Dulr. [*Mimicking.*] Fee-e-ling!

Lett. With a vengeance! [*Extricating herself, with a show
of anger.*] You are very free, Mr. Dulruse.

Dulr. I always am, my dear; quite at home with such pretty
rogues as you. Delicious song, that, — must have left quite a
bouquet on your lips: let me taste it. [*Attempting to kiss her.*

Lett. [*Boxing his ears violently.*] There; take that! And if
you 're so fond of *bouquets*, sir, you 'd better let Miss Mildmay
furnish you: you 'll find too many thorns about my posy.

Dulr. Hark you, child! you may think yourself vastly
witty; but, let me tell you, you are devilish saucy.

Lett. I came to look for Miss Clairvoir's fan, not to meet
you. And now I 've found it, I wish you more manners, and a
good afternoon. [*Curtsies contemptuously, and is about to leave
the room. Dulr. lays hold of her arm, and, in their struggles, he
comes with his back against the door and closes it.*] Let me go,
sir: you 'd better, for your own reputation.

Dulr. Yours, you mean. The door is now shut, hussy;
and, if you 'd have me forgive that blow, you 'll leave these
airs for your betters.

Lett. My betters, sir! And who are they? Not you, nor
your mother, I can tell you. Let me go.

Dulr. You are very pert.

Lett. You are very impertinent.

Dulr. For a chambermaid, my little blackeyed vixen, you
have —

Lett. — Too much penetration, not to see through such a
shallow ditch as you.

Dulr. Come, come! my angel of the bedquilts; though your
eyes do flash fire —

Lett. — They would find it hard to inflame such a mouldy
bit of tinder, as you are. And so — [*struggling.*

Dulr. — Take that, Miss Impudence. [*Trying to kiss her.*

Lett. No; that, Mr. Fool! [*Thrusting the fan in his face.*

Dulr. Curse it, you minx; this is carrying the joke too far.

Lett. No farther, sir, than Miss Clairvoir did for you a minute ago. [*Dulr. in confusion, lets go her arm. Lett. opens the
door.*] — You have a high notion of your own capacity, Mr.
Dulruse; three women at once. And yet, let me tell you,
you have n't heart enough for one of them, though you have
effrontery enough for all three. [*He springs at her. She darts
through the doorway. Then, seeing him pause, Lett. puts back
her head into the room.*] And now, hear a last word, sir, —
which, for your sake, more than my own, I wont speak as
loud as you obliged Miss Clairvoir to do: — He that has n't
wit enough to make the mistress listen, need not think to come
over the maid; and the man that is so base as to cheat one lady,
and lie to another, is just worthy to attempt the honor of a
poor servingmaid, but is too contemptible to put it ever in peril.
Good day, sir. [*Curtsies low, and Exit, singing significantly, —
while he stands unable to move, from confusion and rage:*]

—— " but my feelings I smother:

O *thou* hast been the cause of this *anguish*, my *Mother!* "

Dulr. [*After a moment.*] Bit on every side, by Heaven!
[*Exit, clenching his hands.*

Scene III.

[23] *St. John's Square. The enclosure is seen.*

Enter,
on the outside, Walton, *walking leisurely, and,*
in the opposite direction, Gantelet.
Gantelet, *as he comes in front of* Walton, *touches*
his hat respectfully ; Walton *returns the*
salute, and is about to pass, but checks himself suddenly.

Walt. So, Gantelet ; is that you?

Gant. Aat Monsieur Waltone sareveece. [*Bowing.*

Walt. Your master has returned then?

Gant. No, sare ; Monsieur Rantolph haav stop aat Philadelphie.

Walt. And sent you on. I should not have thought, my
good Gantelet, that he could have spared you.

Gant. [*Bowing humbly.*] Monsieur is ver' complaison' : de
pauvre Gantelet is note really wort' notting.

Walt. When does he return?

Gant. Dis eveneeng, sare : he stay aat Philadelphie for soam
Vol. V.—3

leetel affaire, soam *bagatelle*, and senda me on, in de mornıng, wid all hees effaics — hees baags, hees portmanteau, hees *fusil*, hees every ting.

Walt. Did you leave Mr. Racy at his lodgings?

Gant. *Non, monsieur.* Ah! I me recall in dis *moment*, Monsieur Raacie waas gone out, all *exprès* for to saw Monsieur Waltone.

Walt. To see me? When? how long ago?

Gant. Wan, two, tree minoot; ver' leetel vile.

Walt. How unfortunate! I was just going to him. Well, if you should meet him, Gantelet, tell Mr. Racy, that he will find me at his lodgings.

Gant. *Oui, monsieur.* [*He touches his hat respectfully, as Walton moves on, and is about to depart in the opposite direction, when*

Enter LETTY,
in great haste, from the side at which Gantelet first appeared, i.e., facing Walton. She moves directly up to the latter ; and Gantelet stops to watch the meeting.

Lett. O, Mr. Walton ; I am so rejoiced to meet you, sir !

Walt. Well, Letty ; what is the matter ? Take breath. You need not wait, Gantelet. [*Gant., behind Walton's back, shakes his fist at Letty, who smiles in return maliciously. Exit Gant.*

Lett. Oh, sir, I have just been, as fast as I could go, to Mr. Racy's, and not finding him at home, I thought I would take the liberty to go to you; and I am so glad I have met you, sir! There have been such doings at our house! [*Fans her-self with her apron.*

Walt. What? Quick!

Lett. Why, sir, there is Miss Mildmay, all in tears, poor thing! and Miss Catharine — [*Fanning.*

Walt. For Heaven's sake!

Lett. — So distressed! I beg pardon. You must know, Mr. Walton, that Mr. Clairvoir —— I really don't know how to tell you, sir.

Walt. Letty! this is worse than murder: speak out, at once.

Lett. Then, sir, the truth is, the devil is in the matter. [*Un-tying the strings of her bonnet, and fanning violently.*] Mr. Clairvoir has actually forbid Miss Catharine to think any more about you.

Walt. You dream.

Lett. I wish I did, sir; and that we all did; but the only dreamers are Miss Catharine's father and Mrs. Dulruse; and that wretch, Mrs. Dulruse, is at the bottom of the whole business.

Walt. Go on, go on; though I scarcely can believe you.

Lett. Yet it is true, sir. It seems that you have said something about their silly magnetism that has displeased the old gentleman. [24] He and the housekeeper have been talking about it over and over again this afternoon. What was said, I don't know; but suddenly Mr. Clairvoir comes out of the room, crying out, in a very determined tone, "I'll do it": he sees me on the stairs, tells me to call Miss Catharine: they had a conversation together; I felt uneasy; I could n't resist entering the room; and I heard Mr. Clairvoir tell Miss Cath-

arine "that she was not to think of you any more, but he
would provide a husband that had more brains, and was more
worthy of her." Excuse me, sir; they are his words, no ideas
of mine.

Walt. Never mind; go on.

Lett. The rest, sir, is very little. The old gentleman leaves
the room, and I went out too; and before I got up stairs, I
saw Mr. Dulruse go in. Now you must know, sir — But
—— No, it's right that I should tell you. — Mr. Dulruse,
sir, has been making love to Miss Clairvoir for more than a
week past. O, dear Mr. Walton! don't look so pale about it:
do you think Miss Catharine would think of such a thing as
he! Lor', sir, he is beneath my contempt, let alone such a lady
as Miss Clairvoir's.

Walt. But Catharine never told me!

Lett. No indeed; she is not one of those ladies that love to
have gentlemen fight about them. Had you heard what she
said to Mr. Dulruse, at this last interview, like a high-spirited
lady as she is, you would not feel concern on that score.

Walt. True, true indeed: I don't know how I could be so
weak, as to think for a moment ——

Lett. Lord, sir! there he is! [*While Walton and Letty have
been talking, two or three persons have crossed the scene, and, at
last, Dulruse. He looks at the party suspiciously, and passes on,
just as Letty notices him.*

Walt. Where? who? Ah! [*About to spring after Dulr.
Letty stops him.*

Lett. For Heaven's sake, Mr. Walton! Think of Miss Catharine. And for such a man!

Walt. You are right; let him go.   You are a good and sensible girl, Letty.   What next?

²⁵ *Lett.* O sir, don't flatter me, or I shall begin to think all men alike.   Mr. Dulruse has been complimenting me at a prodigious rate, I can tell you, sir, — and I mean to tell somebody else too.

Walt. What! a general lover?   But that is none of my business.

Lett. No, sir?   I should have thought it was.   But you and Miss Catharine have such high notions of delicacy, you never will listen to other people's secrets.

Walt. Nor should you either, Letty.   But you are a good girl   [*Offering her money.*]   A shawl, or a ring or two.

Lett. No, sir; thank you; I have my pride, as well as my betters. Wait till your wedding-day.   Come, you are going to flatter me again, Mr. Walton: don't turn my head. —   Well, sir, to finish my story, and quickly; for people are beginning to look at us: —   When Mr. Dulruse had done with the mistress, he comes to make love to the maid, though I believe he was in search of his mother.   I gave him his dismissal, as quickly as Miss Catharine had done, (you need not smile; I did, sir,) and then, without saying a word to anybody, I put on my things, and ran all the way to Miss Catharine's uncle's; for I knew, if anybody could help her, it was Mr. Racy; and I think it high time he should interfere.   Speak of the — old boy! — I do declare, here he is.

Enter RACY.

Racy. Eh, what the devil, Schuyler!   Making love to my

little Letty ? Too bad that ! Hark you, child ; don't you let him teach you nonsense.

Lett. Not such a child as you take me for, Mr. Racy ; and if I was, I would n't come to an old widower for instruction. [*Curtsies coquettishly.*

Racy. You imp ! [*Drives her off.*

Lett. [*Coming back.*] Oh, Mr. Walton, please tell this old gentleman what I told you ; but, pray, for Miss Catharine's sake, — don't let him teach you wickedness. [*Exit.*

Racy. Ha, ha, ha ! give an inch, you know. O, the devil ! I forget we 're in the street. I wonder what makes all the girls so free with me, Schuyler ; eh, boy ? From the mistress to the maid, they say just what they please to old Frank Racy.

Walt. They know his good-nature.

Racy. What, what ! Now that 's but half what you mean ; there is something more in the corners of your mouth. No matter. I say, Walt ; do you know I was seeking you ?

Walt. And I was in search of you.

Racy. Well, that 's odd ; but, I 'll bet you a supper, I 've the best news. Frank Randolph 's got back from Richmond ! he will be here in an hour, you dog : his *Parlez-vous* came on this morning with all his luggage. There 's news for you, Long-legs ! Gad ! we 'll have a night of it. Why, how devilish grave you look ! What is in the wind, now ?

Walt. Let us walk on, and I 'll tell you. Your niece ——

Racy. What, what ! I might have looked for some cursed catastrophe, when a waitingmaid was in the plot. [*Puts his arm through Walton's.*] Well, well, my niece ? [*Exeunt.*

ACT THE THIRD

SCENE I. *The housekeeper's apartment at Mr. Clairvoir's.*

DULRUSE *walking up and down in great heat;* MRS. D.
following, and expostulating with him.

Mrs. D. But, Arnold, — Arnold dear ——

Dulr. Mother, you talk like a fool. I tell you, your fine
schemes will amount to nothing. Do you think you can keep
up such a paltry farce as your magnetism much longer? Even
if you could hope to always humbug the old man, there 's his
half-brother Racy, (whom I hate as I do poison!) and that
proud puppy, Walton, and that madcap nephew of Racy's
wife, his adopted son, Frank Randolph I mean, who, coxcomb
though he is, is as shrewd as his uncle, and quite as fearless,
folk say, — how the devil are you to manage all these? Are
you going to blind *them?* and do you think that they wont
open Clairvoir's eyes? I tell you, you 'll be blown up; and I
may get a bullet through my gizzard, for listening to your
deused nonsense. I wish, old woman, [26] you had left me contented with the ten-thousand, and the pretty thing that was
willing to bestow it upon me. You have made me go further,
and you 'll find I shall fare worse. The devil take your ma-
nœuvering !

Mrs. D. But my darling, my baby! ——

Dulr. Yes, you have made a baby of me. I wish you had been gagged with the clout,[27] before you had sung to sleep my reason. Huffed by the mistress, laughed-at by the maid! —— Look you, mother, I have n't yet told you: I met that impertinent vixen, Letty, not half-an-hour ago, in close parley with Walton; and, as I passed them, I heard my name mentioned. Now, what do you say? Walton would never stand talking in the street with a maidservant, unless there was something of moment. What do you say to that, my cunning mamma?

Mrs. D. Why, I 'll get before them, that 's all.

Dulr. That 's all! Hum! that 's a good deal, you will find. And, pray, how do you mean to do that?

Mrs. D. Don't talk so loud. By making you marry Miss Clairvoir at once. There!

Dulr. There? There? Why, you 're crazy, old woman.

Mrs. D. Am I, you undutiful wretch? Am I? Then manage your business yourself.

Dulr. [*Looking at her with surprise.*] Why, you don't mean to tell me —— You 've some scheme in your head, I see; a deused foolish one, I dare say; but let us hear it.

Mrs. D. It would serve you right ——

Dulr. Come, don't palaver.

Mrs. D. Could you run away with Catharine?

Dulr. Ha, ha! I have legs; and so has she: but how are you going to make her use them for my benefit? You 're a wise one!

Mrs. D. This way. Just have a little patience. Suppose

she made a mistake, and took you for Walton; you 're pretty much of a size; and in the dark, you know? ——

Dulr. Why, you 're mad; you 've got this scheme out of some silly storybook. Do girls go off in the dark now-a-days, and marry a fellow without looking at him?

Mrs. D. Yes, when they 're in a hurry, and can't help themselves.

Dulr. [*Turning with great quickness.*] Eh! what? [*Looking at her sharply.*] Speak out.

Mrs. D. Why, look here. I 've so worked upon old Clairvoir that he has actually forbid his daughter to speak of Walton, and swears she shall have you. —

Dulr. Yes, yes, I know that already: but she wont have me, I tell you; and by and by, old Clairvoir comes to his senses.

Mrs. D. [*chuckling.*] When it 's too late. Look here, my darling: suppose I go to Miss Catharine, and make b'lieve side with her, and persuade her to run off with Walton?

Dulr. Ah! Go on, go on.

Mrs. D. She consents; you manage to take Walton's place ——

Dulr. Very easy that, to be sure! And suppose I could, do you think, when she came to find me out, she would —— But stop! stop; a light breaks in upon me. Don't interrupt me. [*Stamps on the floor, and makes his mother fall back. He meditates.*] By the gods! I have it; I 've finished your plot;[28] I have it. Look here, mother. I will pretend to give up my pretensions to Catharine, and make my peace with Mary, which is easily done. You tell Catharine that I have

3*

done so, and that I will run off with Mary, at the same time that she does with Walton, but in a different carriage. No, no! curse it! that wont do either. Stay! [*Thinks again.*] O! You shall let Miss Clairvoir know that I have *not* given up my pretensions, — *not*, remember; but you will say that you pity Mary, and are resolved that I shall not be so false — Yes, that's what fools call it; never mind abusing me. Tell her that if she will change dresses with Mary, who, you know, is just her height, that I shall take Mary for her, and run off with her, while she in Mary's dress is really gone off with Walton.

Mrs. D. Yes, but what good will that do you?

Dulr. Are you such a fool? Why I sha'n't do any such thing, to be sure, but take the real fifty-thousand, and, when we are in the carriage — I'll[29] personate her lover without talking, and make her glad enough to have me, or anybody else, before we get to the parson.

Mrs. D. But, Arny dear, that will be too wicked. —

Dulr. Scruples? and from you, mother? Your tricks are not so bold, to be sure, but they're quite as bad.

Mrs. D. No; they're not. Besides, why can't you tell her that her lover is false, and gone off knowingly with Mary; then she'll marry you, you know, out of revenge.

Dulr. No doubt [*sneeringly.*]. Well, well, mother; I'll do so. We'll trot off to Harlem; and before we're half way to the parsonage, I'll be bound that I convince her.

Mrs. D. And to-morrow, I'll persuade old Clairvoir to have me without running away. Buss me, Arny: we'll fix 'em.

Dulr. Pshaw! there. [*giving her his cheek, disdainfully.*]

Now, be off, and ply Miss Clairvoir well. I 'll stay here till you come back. Don't forget now, *she* is to dress like Mary, to deceive *me:* remember, don't spare me.

Mrs. D. Yes, yes; leave me alone; I 'm a wise one. [*Exit.*

Dulr. [*Closing the door.*] Ay, ay. My father must have been a wiser, or I don't know where I came from. [*As the door shuts, the scene changes to*

Scene II.

The Drawing-room, as in Act I. Scene I.

Catharine, *seated in a thoughtful attitude.* Enter Letty.

Lett. Miss Catharine.

Cath. Well, Letty.

Lett. Mrs. Dulruse begs permission to speak a few words to you.

Cath. To me? Let her come in.

Lett. Yes, ma'am. But — [*Going up to Cath., and lowering her voice.*] Miss Catharine — a horrible plot — but don't let her know you see into it. Listen to her, dear Miss Catharine — and, if you can, pretend to consent — but don't believe a word she says.

Cath. What is this? I hope, Letty, you have not been listening again.

Lett. O ma'am, I cannot tell you all now; never mind how

I know. If I stay longer, she 'll suspect. Only promise me, that you 'll not be too candid: you know I do all for the best.

Cath. Well, well, Letty; we 'll talk of this again. I 'll be careful.

Lett. Thank you, Miss Catharine. Don't look at her too sharply! [*Exit.*

Cath. Plot! [*She becomes again thoughtful. After a few minutes,*

Enter *Mrs.* DULRUSE.

Mrs. D. Miss Clairvoir —

Cath. Oh! Sit down, madam. Is there anything particular?

Mrs. D. Yes, I —— But let me shut the door. Now, Miss Clairvoir — I — really — I hope, ma'am, you don't believe I have a bad heart?

Cath. If I do believe so, Mrs. Dulruse, it will be easy for you to prove I am in the wrong.

Mrs. D. That 's the very thing I came for, Miss Catharine. Now — let me see — now, you know, Miss Catharine, your father has been pleased to favor certain —— If you look so cold at me, I can't go on.

Cath. I see no reason, ma'am, why I should look otherwise.

Mrs. D. [*From this moment, she talks without turning her face to Cath.*] Well, I 'll tell you then, why you should. I 'm your friend, Miss Catharine; and I don't like it at all, that your father has chose to favor my Arnold's pertensions.

Cath. Indeed.

Mrs. D. Yes; and I so pity your poor cousin.

Cath. Miss Mildmay, ma'am, needs not your pity.

Mrs. D. O, Miss Clairvoir, but she does; for I know she loves my Arnold; and Arnold I know might have loved her; but, now he has his head turned by higher notions ——

Cath. Mrs. Dulruse!

[20] *Mrs. D.* Do let me finish, Miss Catharine. I was coming to tell you that I don't approve my boy's falsehood. He is a base, wicked, unnatural wretch! Yes, that he is! and I don't want to draw down the judgment of Providence by aidin' and abettin' him. So, Miss Clairvoir, if you want to cheat your papa, and marry Mr. Walton after all, I'll help you.

Cath. I don't know what ideas you have of me, Mrs. Dulruse; but I am not in the habit of cheating my father in anything; and, as for my marriage, I do not see that you have anything to do with it.

Mrs. D. O Lord! you take a body's words up so! I was only going to say, if you would listen, ma'am, that I know a way, you could put a stop to Arnold's persumption, make Miss Mary happy, and yourself, and — and — everybody.

Cath. Indeed? Well.

Mrs. D. You see, nothing can be done openly, while the old man —

Cath. Mr. *Clairvoir*, — if you mean my father.

Mrs. D. Excuse me — yes — while Mr. Clairvoir is so violent against Mr. Walton. But if you would run away with Mr. Walton, you know — [*Cath. looks at her with surprise and attention; Mrs. D., however, still keeping her head turned away.*] why then it would be too late. Now I have such a darling little plot, [31] which my Arn — I mean, which 'll make

Arnold behave himself. You engage your cousin to run off
with Arnold; Arnold 'll be ready, and Mr. Walton will be
ready too; but you put on your cousin's dress, and make her
put on yours. Then Arny, you know, will think that she is
you, and take her off, and marry her out of hand, as he ought,
shame on him! while you and Mr. Walton 'll go another way.
[*Ringing within.*] There's somebody: will you think of my
little plan, Miss Clairvoir, and tell me, by 'n 'by?

Cath. Yes, yes, I 'll think on it.

Mrs. D. It 'll be just like a play. Everybody 'll be so happy.
[*Cath. walks away. Mrs. D. bridles, turns up her nose, curtsies,
looks maliciously at her.*] Hum! [*Exit, strutting. — Cath.
stands thoughtful, for a few moments. Then*

Enter
RACY, *preceded by* LETTY *running.*

Lett. Here's Mr. Racy, Miss Catharine. I 've told him all.
O! I 'm so delighted!

Racy. Out, slyboots! mind your place. [*Driving her off.
Exit Letty.*] Well, Kate, here 's been rare plotting, eh! But
we 'll outplot them; we 'll countermine their mine, my
beauty!

Cath. I think I guess what you mean, uncle, from Letty's
hints, and that foolish woman's awkwardness.

Racy. Foolish enough; but not the less rogue, for all that.
But we 'll match them! I wish the hour were only come: I
long to be at it.

Cath. At what, uncle? There's a plot, I see: but I am not

so silly as to fall into the snare. You need not fear me; I shall not run off.

Racy. Yes, but you will though; and Walton shall run off too; and so shall Mary, and that scamp, Dulruse; ay, and his precious mother after him. Gad! you wench, there shall be such a carrying-off, as has never been heard of since the rape of Proserpine.

Cath. But, uncle ——

Racy. Don't butt at me, niece, or you 'll hurt that little head of yours. What, what! here have I the rarest counterplot in the world, and was going to make you and Schuyler happy, and Mary happy, and those two devils unhappy — as they ought to be, and your father a wise man, and — and —— Damn it! I 'll do it — wont hear scruples — not a word, not a word.

Cath. I dare not deceive my father, uncle.

Racy. But I dare, and will undeceive him afterwards. And there 's that puss, Mary; I mean to undeceive her too.

Cath. Yet you would have her run off with —

Racy. — That rascal Arnold? Sure, sure; nothing so effectual to undeceive her; nothing. Dont you see it, you hussy? You used to have so bright a wit; but you and Walton are grown the stupidest people, since you have taken to cooing! Well, that blush is a rare embellisher, — sha'n't quarrel with you. But hark you, Kate; do you think that if Arnold find he has carried off the ten-thousand, when he thought he had the fifty, he will be in any hurry to conclude the bargain? By the Lord, no! And he never shall, at any rate. How would you like your cousin to be disgusted with the traitor?

Cath. Nothing could render me happier.

Racy. There you — You make a mistake there, you slut; but I know it will render you very happy. And how would you like a fine, hearty, whole-souled fellow for Mary's husband; just such another as myself, only a little handsomer, and a good deal younger, eh?

Cath. I should be delighted, indeed; for she deserves one.

Racy. And she shall have one; and money in his purse, into the bargain. There; that will do: I must now go and arrange matters with Walton. You 'll be ready to-night, about ten o'clock?

Cath. But uncle, dear uncle ——

Racy. Not one word — not one syllable. I 'll send Schuyler to you, with arguments in plenty. Settle it between you. I believe the devil is in me, when I get a plot in my head; for I 'm as happy as —— O, by the by, Letty made me promise her your forgiveness. She 's been eavesdropping, the wench; but it was all for your good. What, what! displeased? Wont have it — too scrupulous — circumstances alter cases — go to your cousin — there — there [*Pushing her out. of the door, while she endeavors vainly to speak.*] — there! Out with you; talk to Mary: I 'll after Schuyler. [*Exeunt.*

ACT THE FOURTH

SCENE I. *Racy's lodgings.*

Randolph's dressing-room. — A couch, wardrobe, and dressing-
table. A magnificent cheval-glass.   Other
mirrors, and articles of the toilet of a costly and elegant
description. GANTELET, arranging the things on
the dressingtable, occasionally smelling affectedly at the essence-
bottles, and admiring himself in the glass.

Gant. [*Singing, in a subdued voice.*

> " Allons, enfans de la patrie !
> Le jour de gloire est arrivé " — [32]

Enter RACY.

Racy. It is, eh ? So I should think. And you are keeping
it very mellifluously, you jackdaw.

Gant. [*who, while Racy is speaking, has been making several
humble bows, by way of apology.*] *Pardon,* Monsieur Raacie ;
your *pauvre serviteur* note know dat you waas *présent.*

Racy. And where 's your master ? Not come yet ?

Gant. Ah, *oui,* yase — dat is, no ; he come all de hour.
[*Noise within, as of a carriage stopping.*] *Ah, le voilà !* dere
he is ! [*noise, as of the steps let down.*

Racy. Gad! *my boy!* [*These two words in a tone of deep emotion, while he looks eagerly at the open door.*

Some one is heard approaching, singing gaily :

> " Amici, il ciel pietoso
> Le vostre preci accolga! —— 33

Enter RANDOLPH.

Racy. You have your wish for once, you dog; for I have been praying, for this hour, to see that impudent face of yours; and maybe some other fools have been equally pious.

Rand. Ah, nuncle! Kiss me, old boy! [*Kisses Racy on one cheek.*] Now, t' other; *à la Française.* [*Kisses him on the other, while Racy pishes and pshaws, and endeavors to escape.*] But where the devil did you learn Italian?

Racy. There 's a rascal for you! Why, you unnatural cur! where did you learn it? Did n't you have your first lesson from me? the original taste, you coxcomb?

Rand. Yes, and the draught was so oddly qualified, that I never knew whether it was of the real Tuscan grape, or downright Hollands, — till a *prima donna* taught me the difference.

Racy. By a very moral intoxication, doubtless. Mere detraction! *Prima donna,* indeed, you affected fop! And what might your erudition have gained by her *solfegging ?*

Rand. A pleasant piece of knowledge, most usually learned from such *maéstrè :* that the *diminuendo* of my pocket needed no straining, while the *crescendo* of my conscience —

Racy. Was always an effort.

Rand. A very natural progression, on *mi sol!* [34]

Racy. O base pun! If the tenor of your wisdom must run off into this falsetto, your years will find their treble a choice part in the opera of folly.

Rand. Bravo, uncle! you run counter to your own instructions, like many other preachers.

Racy. Ay, the dogs are sadly fond of *ad libitum* passages.

Rand. But to leave these sharps, and come to the flats at home —

Racy. Videlicet, my half-brother, and Madam Dulruse. Ah! you young hound, I have the rarest sport in cover for you! and a bit of special game besides, that will make your mouth water: such a doe! But first, how did you find the folk in the Old Dominion?

Rand. Tough as ever, and transported of course to see your humble servant. Such a round of feasting! And that infernal Barbecue-Club! I have nearly drunk my liver into a hepati'tis. Aunt Peggy, though, was very rabid about these innocents [*coaxing his mustaches.*], and vowed I looked more like a ramcat than a human being: think of the savage of the Blue Ridge! But I 'm revenged on her atrocity: the old panther would have me bring you a spongecake of her own composition, enveloped in a ream of letter-paper: I pitched it to a beggar on the road, — the fellow looked so devilish hungry. It would have done your heart good to see his astonishment: I thought, nunc', he would never have shut his mouth.

Racy. Out, you crackbrain! was that the way to treat your aunt? my property too! [*Shaking him, but with a look of fondness and admiration.*

Rand. Pshaw! what the deuse do you want of sponge-cake?   No matter, *mio caro ;* I 've something better for you: Aunt Sally has sent you a flannel nightcap to keep your head warm, and sister Betsy has knit you six pairs of woolen stockings, against the winter; the dear souls say you will be wanting them, for the rheumatism.

Racy. What, what! You lie, you lie. But what detained you in Philadelphia? Fanny Ellsler?

Rand. Fanny — Ell — sler! *Che questio'ne curio'sa!* [35] She never shows her legs, you know, till evening. And then, have I not seen Taglioni's toes? *Pote'r di soc'co!* you might as well tell me of some simple tenor of Ber'gamo, when I have been rapt into the seventh heaven of ecstacy on the breath of Rubini.

Racy. Or of old Frank Racy, when you have been drinking Tuscan from the enchanted cup of some Circe of the opera.

Rand. [*In a natural manner.*] No, dear uncle, now you wrong me! [*Putting his arm affectionately about Racy's waist, and gently hugging him.*] Do I not owe everything to you? Though there is not a drop of your blood in my veins (as, on my soul, I wish it was all yours!) have you not been my instructor, friend, uncle, father, all to me? You dear, good soul, you! you are worth a thousand primadonnas, though Malibran herself was of them!

Racy. [*Turning aside, with emotion, and wiping his eyes: while Gantelet takes snuff.*] Plague on your nonsense! Can't you keep your collar out of my eye?

Rand. [*Going to the cheval-glass.*] Now tell me, nunc', what is all this game you have on foot for me? [*Takes a small mir-*

ror in his hand — brushes carefully and slowly his mustaches and whiskers — then lays down the mirror and parts his long curled hair [36] *with his fingers, &c. &c.*

Racy. [*After watching his movements, for a moment, with a droll expression of mingled wonder, humor, and vexation.*] Was there ever such a puppy! — Would any one believe that this fellow could back a horse with the best man in Virginia, fence like a Neapolitan, put a pistol-bullet through a card-spot at thirty paces, and shoot flying with Leatherstocking? Come away from that glass! I 've no patience.

Rand. [*Singing falsetto. With affected melancholy and anxiety.*] " Deh! ti calma! " [37]

Racy. Calm myself! you Miss-Nancy! I 'll have you married; I will: your wife shall singe your smellers, and [38] Delilize your locks to make frizettes.

Rand. [*Still before the glass.*] They are no longer in fashion, uncle.

Racy. No, the women have resigned their frivolities to the men : they dress their brainpans classically, and 't is you, the breeches-wearers, that have turned Goths. Is this the fruit of your three years' travel in the old world? to wear long ringlets like a girl, and —— Confound you, sir! you left us a fellow of some sense : what have you returned? An Adonis, a Narcissus, an Hermaphrodi'tus.

Rand. [*Bowing to his uncle, in the glass.*] *Ella mi va lusingándo* [39] : they were beauties. But your story, *zio mio*, your story.

Racy. Hum! I scarcely know whether such a thing, as you, is worth trusting with it. But we are not alone.

Rand. Gaut, leave us. [*Gant. bows and is going off.*] The fellow, though, is trustworthy.

Racy. I have heard you say so before. And we may want him. Come back, you Gantelet.

Gant. À Monsieur Raacie's sareveece.

Racy. Can you keep a secret for three whole hours?

Gant. [*Putting his hand on his heart, and bowing.*] Monsieur does me too mush honneur: trya me.

Racy. Well, stand aside. Now, Frank, do you know what Animal Magnetism is?

Rand. [*Throwing himself at full length on the couch.*] O, a sensible doctrine, that teaches us that a blind woman, or an idiot, has more brains than Benjamin Franklin, and that a twopenny quack, with a trick of his thumbs, can do what George the Third with all his armies could not, — control the will in others, and give a forcible direction to thought.

Racy. My brother, Hal Clairvoir, has become a convert.

Rand. You don't say so?

Racy. And in order to have a race of magnetic children, whose eyes shall be where their mouths should, and who shall talk with their stomachs, he is going to marry Mother Dulruse himself, and force Kate to pig with the son.

Rand. [*Springing to his feet.*] The devil! And what becomes of Schuyler Walton?

Racy. He's to be dismissed, because he will not dismiss his senses. Now, the Dulruses,[40] fearing that their influence will not last many days, have got up a fine scheme for a runaway marriage, by which that rascal Arnold is to get Kate, and Schuyler to be turned over to Mary, under pretence of doing just the contrary. But I 've reversed the tables: we are going to have the frolic; but the biter is to be bitten.

Rand. How? And leave that sweet girl Mary to that artful villain?

Racy. No, no; not quite, not quite: I 've another partner preparing for her.

Rand. Ha, ha!

[*Singing.*] " Unisco le famiglie,
Le liti io rendo nulle,
E spesso alle fanciulle } *twice.* [41]
Marito soglio dar."

Racy. Do leave Rossini for a moment, will you? She 's a capital wench, eh Frank?

Rand. Who? Rossini? Never tried her.

Racy. Can't you be quiet? Mary, Mary.

Rand. Mary? Oh yes; a devilish good girl; but rather tame.

Racy. No, no; you mistake her character: she 's not so volatile as her cousin, but she has mind and soul as well as beauty. You must have seen her often since your return from Europe: — does she please you?

Rand. E cómè! [42]

Racy. Then you shall have her, with my blessing, and — something else.

Rand. Pian, piano! I 'm in no hurry for a wife.

Racy. Well, well. — Must have you, at any rate, to help us in this affair. Can you play Jarvie?

Rand. Anything to pleasure you. Which number, if your honor plases? The white house is it, sir? All right, yer honor. Tuck! tuck! git up, ye blind deevil!

Racy. Pshaw, pshaw! you 're not to be the whip. You shall mount the box merely for precaution : for when that rogue, Dulruse, shall find he is sailing off with the wrong prize, he 'll be apt to turn pirate in earnest, and show all his brutality.

Rand. Let him : I 'll whip him! ——

Racy. No, no; I wont have that. Interfere to protect Mary ; but let us have no whipping.

Rand. That 's a pity. But I 'll find a way to —— When is this rape to begin ?

Racy. By ten to-night, at furthest.

Rand. To-night ? *Avéte sem'pre fúria.*[43] It cannot be.

Racy. But it must; for the chief object is to undeceive Mary ; and that never will be, till we throw Arnold off his guard.

Rand. Amen, then. But let us hear your plan in full.

Racy. By and by; no time, now. Oh! there is another part of the play not yet allotted. I should like to open Hal 's eyes so wide, that they will never close again on this imposture ; but I don't want to run away with Mother Dulruse myself.

Rand. Ha, ha, ha! I should like to see you.

Racy. You would, would you ? I think not. Now, could I find somebody that would get the start of brother Clairvoir ——

Rand. Well, what?

Racy. The old fool is so eager, I believe she could be persuaded to give him the slip, rather than wait.

Rand. What a pity she cannot serve herself, as authors now-a-days manage a dull novel, divide her unity into numbers, eh? She might pass with some *éclat*, where, taken in the volume, the composition is insufferable.

Racy. Well, well; but we cannot make a polypus of *her;* one head must answer. I could do the job myself; for the tender creature's *Ready for Anybody*, and has made love to me furiously for a long time; but I would rather find a substitute.

Rand. Stay! I know one.

Racy. The deuse you do! Where? Who?

Rand. There is a Neapolitan that came over in the same vessel with me. I know him to be needy, and unscrupulous. What is more, he makes no ceremony of acknowledging it. He is cold, resolute, intelligent, an open scoffer at everything divine and human, and all with the gravest face in the world. He is genteel enough looking," has been an officer of Napoleon's, and wears the red ribbon, — and sports mustaches a yard long. A sum of money would make him pass himself off, on the old dame, for a count or marquis, or for the Pasha of Egypt, if you prefer; and ——

Racy. Bravo! the brightest scheme.

Rand. But it will take time.

Racy. No, no; it shall be done at once. A count could persuade the old fool in ten minutes. Where is this desperado? But, I hope, my boy, you don't associate with him? [*seriously.*

Rand. God forbid! I know, though, where to find him. Here, Gantelet; do you recollect the Italian gentleman?

Gant. The monsieur wid de grand *moustache?* *Oui, monsieur,* ver' vell: *belle figure. teint basané.*

Rand. Yes, — good looking, — swarthy complexion. You 'll

find him at Palmo's [45] always at this hour. Go there, and tell him that Mr. Randolph would see him on business of importance without delay. Run all the way; or jump into a 'bus.

Gant. [*Going.*] *Oui, monsieur.*

Racy. Stop! Can't we have a supper here, Frank, in an hour?

Rand. Why yes, if you want it. What for?

Racy. To bring Dulruse to the point I wish. The rogue is passionate: he shall have just wine enough to put him off his guard.

Rand. Good! Gantelet, stop at Windust's [46] on your way, and tell him to send down, within an hour, supper for — how many, uncle?

Racy. We'll have Walton and the Count: five.

Rand. Supper for five; an elegant one. What wines?

Racy. Never mind them. There's the old stock; and I have some dozens of that Hiedsieck left, thanks to your absence.

Rand. O! I thought I had been longer away.

Racy. You rascal! [*Beating him.*

Rand. Off, Gant. Be back immediately — shall want to send you with a letter to Mrs. Dulruse.

Gant. Oui, monsieur : I flies. [*Exit Gant.*

Racy. What's that? what letter?

Rand. From the Count, to be sure, declaring his passion, and supplicating for an instant interview.

Racy. What, what! Why, you're unmatchable at an intrigue. You have had other lessons abroad besides musical ones, you dog. Does your count talk good English?

Rand. Uncommonly good; rather elegant, though with a

foreign accent. He 'll fit her, I warrant you : only do you fit him.

Racy. Never fear. — Must now find Walton, to prepare him. Had great difficulty to bring him to reason. Indeed, but to disenchant Mary, he never would have consented to this deption.

Rand. Ay, ay ; he 's as open as the day, and the very soul of honor.

Racy. And the model of a fine gentleman. He wears [47] his hair short, and eschews mustaches. [*Going.*

Rand. Ha, ha! [*Following to the door.*

> [*Sings.*] " E spesso alle fanciulle
> Marito soglio dar."

Au revoir, uncle Hymen. [*Exit Racy, shaking his fist at him.*] A dear, good soul, if there ever was one. — And now, Madam Dorothy Dulruse, I 'll write you such a letter. [*Going to another door.*

> [*Sings.*] " E spesso alle fanciulle
> Marito soglio dar. [*Exit, singing.*
>
> [48] In me ciascun si può fidar." [*heard within.*

Scene closes.

[40] SCENE II.

The Housekeeper's rooms at Mr. Clairvoir's.

DULRUSE,
walking up and down in a brown study.

Enter, Mrs. DULRUSE, *gaily.*

Mrs. D. She 's coming, Arny : now, do speak her kind.

Dulr. Anything, so I am revenged upon Miss Clairvoir. Once my wife! —— Does the girl come willingly ?

Mrs. D. Mary ?

Dulr. Yes, Mary. How stupid you are! Whom else did you mean ?

Mrs. D. That 's true : but you are so impatient, my dear.

Dulr. Well, well; answer me, mother.

Mrs. D. Does she come willing ? No; we have had rare work to persuade her; she 's just such another stickler as her cou-in.

Dulr. Curse her! But I 'll humble her; I will, by Heaven! [*In a lower tone, and clenching his fist.*

Mrs. D. Not Mary, poor thing! She 's humble enough.

Dulr. Who 's talking about Mary ?

Mrs. D. Why, I was; and so was you. Lor'! there 's her steps. Now, do smooth your brow, my baby; for I 've told

the child you was kind o' struck with remorse, and going to
be very fond of her agin.

Dulr. Perhaps I may -- when Walton gets her.

Mrs. D. Hush!

Enter MARY.

Dulr. [*Taking her hand.*] Mary dear, will you forgive me?

Mary. Arnold, I have never borne you malice.   ⁵⁰ I 've been
very, very sorry — yes, unhappy, (for I will not be ashamed
to own it,) — very unhappy, while I thought you were wil-
fully untrue to me; but your mother — has — has ——

Mrs. D. Yes, I told her it was all of the old man's doin',
and ——

Dulr. Don 't interrupt us, my dear mother. [*frowns at her,
aside.*] Go on, Mary.

† *Mary.* I was only going to say, Arnold, that as your mother
has explained every thing, and you yourself, she tells me, are
— are ——

Dulr. Returned to a sense of my duty, my affection, Mary.
Yes, Heaven was pleased for a time to dazzle my senses with
your cousin's fortune——

Mary. [*Faintly, and with dismay.*]   Indeed? I did not
know ——

Dulr. Mother did not tell you all, through a wish to spare
me: but I have been very bad, my dear. I was seduced
by misrepresentations to think that Mr. Clairvoir preferred a
union between me and —— But I hurt you by this confession.
It was a short struggle, my angel; my better nature has tri-

umphed, and I am — all I was before. [*with a bitter smile at Mrs D. — Mary having her eyes cast down.*

Mary. Then, what need of this clandestine step, Arnold; why should we ——

Dulr. Run away, my dear? Because we cannot stay. Have you not had it all explained? It is the only way to put an end to our novel difficulties; and it will make your cousin happy equally with yourself. Hush! here's your uncle.

Enter CLAIRVOIR.

Clair. Mrs. D., I am waiting for you, my dear. What are you doing there with Mary, Arnold?

Dulr. O sir, I am only persuading her to — to be reconciled: and she is, sir. Hush! [*aside to Mary.*

Mary. [*Aside to Dulr.*] O, I cannot bear this! Let me go, Arnold.

Clair. She looks very uneasy. No matter, Mary child; uncle will provide you another husband, and soon. Come, my dear. [*To Mrs. D.*

Mrs. D. Yes, but we a'n't a-going to experiment now, Mr. Clairvoir?

Clair. No, not quite yet. Have a good heart, Mary. [*Exit with Mrs. D.*

Dulr. There, take your uncle's advice, Mary. And don't think any more about it. You see, it is the only way; he is resolute.

Mary. Well, Arnold, I will not oppose you. But I wish it was over. Will you join us in the parlor? [*Going.*

Dulr. Yes, yes. [*Exit Mary, Arnold, shutting the door on her.*] Scrupulous fool! Over? Hum! [*Looking at his watch.*] Two hours more: — and then, Miss Catharine —— [*compressing his lips, and clenching his hands.* — *Exit.*

Scene III.

The drawingroom, — as in Act I. Scene I.

WALTON *and* CATHARINE, *conversing. Then, Enter* MARY, *slowly.*

Cath. [*Running to her, and taking her affectionately round the waist.*] Come, coz., you sha'n't look so sentimental. Mr. Walton has seen Uncle Racy, and is now convinced that the affair is not only justifiable, but is the very best thing we can do.

Walt. Yes, Miss Mary. On one account, I am still reluctant; but I can assure you sincerely, that I believe this little frolic will eventuate most happily, and particularly so for yourself.

Enter RACY.

Racy. [*to Mary.*] What, what! Coying it yet, my little violet? Come, come, all 's well that ends well. Walton,

Bub's still in the dark, eh? But I'm going to make him play off the last of his experiments on the Dulruse, for my particular edification, presently. What's that? [*shuffling of feet within.*] Heyday! what rat's in the other room?

Letty. [*Within, and very loud.*] Let me go, sir! You ha'l better.

Dulr. [*Within, but lower.*] Come, come, don't be a fool. [*Noise as of a door pushed violently and suddenly open; and*

Enter

LETTY, *staggering backward, from the side of the scene opposite the windows, —* DULRUSE, *having hold of her arms, dragged after her.*

Racy. Here's a catastrophe! Why, what the devil are you doing, Mr. Dulruse?

Dulr. Hum! hum! — I — I was trying to persuade her to intercede for me — with her mistress — whose displeasure [*bowing low to Cuth.*] I fear I have too justly incurred.

Letty. [*eagerly.*] A great! —— [*Racy checks her by a sign.*

Racy. [*aside to Walton.*] I b.lieve he lies like the devil. [*Aloud.*] O yes! that's all right enough. Get you gone, Letty, for an ill-natured puss. [*making another sign to her to be silent.*

Letty. [*going.*] Mr. Dulruse, sir, will never take No for an answer. [*Exit.*

Racy. That looks very like understanding the sex, they say, eh Dulruse? But your pardon is made, sir, with the ladies. Oh, child, [*to Mary.*] you must n't look scared; Mr. Dulruse is not deserving of your jealousy, I assure you. And now we're all here, let us make our final arrangements: and then, boys, have with you both to my lodgings! Somebody there will make you right welcome and merry for an hour.

Cath. Who is it, uncle. Not cousin Fran ——

Racy. [*clapping his hand on her mouth.*] Hold your tongue, hussy; don't spoil sport. — Let us adjourn to the other room — Mr. Dulruse's council-chamber. [*aside to Cath.* —
Exeunt Omnes.

Scene IV.

The Diningroom, — as in Act II. Scene II.

Enter Letty, *leading in* Gantelet. *She shuts the door.*

Letty. And now, Monsieur Jackanapes, tell us all about it. So, you are in the plot, eh? They must have been sadly in want of conspirators.

Gant. Oh ver' vell, if you waas so saacy, Mees Laytie, you sha 'n't know notting at all.

Lett. But I will, though: so let me see that letter that you hold behind you. [*struggling to get it from him.*] Hum! here comes the old woman. I 'll punish you for this. [*Going.*

Gant. Vell, can't you-a hide behind de door, *ma chère?* you shaal dare hear all, and see all too, if you likes.

4*

Lett. Talk loud, then.   Hush! here she is.

Enter Mrs. DULRUSE.

Mrs. D. [*to Letty.*]   What are you doing here ?

Lett. No harm, ma'am, I'm sure.   But I can go out, if you want to be alone with the man. [*Exit, bridling.   She draws the door ajar, and stands behind it.*

Mrs. D. Saucy creature!   Did you want to speak to me ?

Gant. Oui, madame.   I haave de honneur to bring-a you one leetel billet-doux from *Monsieur le Comte de Sanscarlin.*

Mrs. D. Who ?   I never heard the name before.

Gant. Ah no, *madame ;* but de Count he often hear of you ; he see you ; he sigh for you ; he die for you : he take-a no rest at all, notting to eat, notting to drink, since he love — *pardon, madame* ——

Mrs. D. Sure, here's some mistake. [*looking pleased.*] Count! A foreign gentleman ?

Gant. Braave foreign *gentilhomme ;* great frent of Monsieur Rantolph.   He see *madame* a — a — I nevare knows where, *mon dieu* — but ver' frakontly.   He beg Monsieur Rantolph to maak him acquaint : Monsieur Rantolph say no.

Mrs. D. Why so ?   That was very ungentlemanly in Mr. Randolph.   I should have been happy, extremely happy to see the count — What is his name, monsheer ?

Gant. Sanzacarlini, *madame ; Comte* Sanzacarlini ; one *Italien ;* fine *gentilhomme ;* reesh, ver' reesh.   Vel, Monsieur Rantolph, *mon jeune maître,* he say to de count : "Vy you no introduce-a yourself?   Write her one billet-doux — filled with fire and flams ; tell her how you die for her ; and run your own reesk. I vont interferes," says Monsieur Rantolph, "vid Meester Clairwar."

Mrs. D. Ah, I see now. Well, I'm sure, the count is a gentleman. Let me see his letter. [*Gant. bows and hands it with great ceremony. Mrs. D. opens it, reads, shows great delight, while Gant. takes the opportunity, her back being turned, to act a little amorous bye-play with Letty, in dumb show.*] — Tell the Count that I will see him — his lordship, as soon as he pleases. Mr. Clairvoir has just stepped out to take his evening walk, and if he will come now, we sha'n't be interrupted.

Gant. He vill come on de vings of Love, *madame;* he vill fly like one grand turkey. [*Exit, snatching a kiss from Letty, as he brushes by her. Letty pushes him off.*

Mrs. D. Heh, heh! What's that? Letty!

Enter LETTY,
leaving the door ajar. GANTELET *is seen to take his place behind it.*

Was that you, Letty?

Lett. Yes, ma'am. That was a very impudent man, madam: he actually kissed me.

Mrs. D. Well, never mind, child. Noblemen's servants will be free. He did n't harm you, I dare say.

Lett. No, ma'am; but I should like to see him do it again. Nobleman, did you say, ma'am?

Mrs. D. Yes, nobleman, Letty: the Count — Count [*reading the letter.*] *Sansercarlini.* Grand name!

Lett. Oh dear! Well, I declare, Mrs. Dulruse; you are the happiest lady; everbody falls in love with you. And did he really write that letter to you?

Mrs. D. To me: see; *Mrs. Dulruse at Mr. Clairvoir's, Broad-way.*[51] [*Showing the superscription.*] If I thought, Letty, that you would n't tell ——

Lett. I tell, ma'am? Lor' ma'am, what do you take me for?

Mrs. D. Well then, shut the door, child.

Lett. Oh ma'am, there 's nobody can hear. However — [*Pushes it a little closer, but still leaves room for Gant. to put his nose through. Mrs. D., the while, gazing with satisfaction on the back of her letter.*

Mrs. D. Now then, you must know, that this great nobleman is a friend of Mr. Francis Racy Randolph's, and ——

Lett. No matter, ma'am; I am so impatient to hear the letter.

Mrs. D. [*Reading.*] *Adorable angel!* Hem! Men will write such foolish things! Do you think I look like an angel, Letty?

Lett. Why, now I look at you, ma'am, I don't know but that you do look a little like one of the three angels I saw in a play once, called *Macbeth.*

Mrs. D. Indeed! Well, that 's odd. [*Reads.*] *Adorable angel!* Flatterer! [*Reads.*] *Persumption though this may be, yours, your beauty's, only, is the fault. I have seen you. Having seen you, I adore you. Adoring you, I must enjoy you.*[52] That 's rather free, Letty.

Lett. Noblemen will be free, ma'am.

Mrs. D. True. [*Reads.*] *I know I have a rival; and that makes me desperate to take these means, instead of waiting for the formality of an introduction. Curse on formality!* How spirited! He's been an orficer. [*Reads.*] *Curse on formality! What is it to the flames with which I burn? Will it put them out?* Poor fellow!

Lett. Yes, he's all afire.

Mrs. D. [*Reading.*] *No, nothing but your sweet presence, your divine language, your super* — su — su — superce — les — yes — *supercelestial condescension will bring about so desirable a conservation.* *Kill me at once* — There's passion for you, Letty! [*Reads.*] *Kill me at once, or let me see you.* *Dying, till I receive your answer; perhaps to die when I do receive it; if not, to live* — oh in ecstacy, ecstati — c, a, l, cal, — yes — *ecstatically ecstatic! I remain, madam, on my bended knees, your afflicted, inconsolable, but not tee-totally* — Oh, he 's heard of the Temperance Society, Letty. But that 's a queer phrase, though.

Lett. You know he 's a foreigner, ma'am.

Mrs. D. So he is. — *Not tee-totally despairing adorer, Count Sanzacarlini, Officer of the Legion of Honor.* Then, in the corner, *To Mrs. Dorothea Dulruse.*

Lett. Well, noblemen really have a delightful style.

Mrs. D. Yes, something so grand, so superlestial. Orficer of a legion of honors! But here 's a *mem.*, Letty. [*Reads.*] *Mem. Perhaps, when you hear me, you may change your intentions, and my rival in his turn may be taught to despair. If he is rich, I am richer* — Think of that, Letty! — *if he is gentle, I am noble ; if he loves you, I — do I not adore you?* [53] *And being younger than he, may I not hope to prove it?* *O prepare to receive me, divine enchantress!* — Lor' s' us! — as *I should be received by one so beautiful and so engaging!* Dear Count! What would you do, Letty, if you was me?

Lett. Why, I would n't tell a soul about it, but keep it all to myself till I had seen the dear man and married him.

Mrs. D. And would you see him, and marry him?

Lett. Yes, if he would have me, marry him at once, run away with him, anything! But take care, ma'am, don't let Mr. Arnold see that! He won't like it, on account of Mr. Clairvoir.

Mrs. D. You 're right, Letty. Well, he sha' n't. You *are* a good-natured thing, I do declare, Letty; and you and I will be very good friends.

Lett. Thank your ladyship, humbly. [*curtsying.*

Mrs D. O now! don't ladyship me yet, Letty; wait till I 'm the Countess, Letty dear. Don't say a word. Countess Sausyleeny, Orficer of a legion of honors! [*Exit, strutting.*

Lett. Ha, ha, ha! Your legionship's humble servant. [*curtsying.*] What an old fool!

Enter GANTELET.

Gant. *Mon dieu!* I vaas nearly run ofer by *Madame* de *Comtesse.*

Lett. Be off now, quick, and tell the impatient Legion to make haste to come and expire at his angel's feet.

Gant. *Ma foi, oui,* or his flams will make hast to expire before him. [*Going.*

Lett. Stop! Do you value my favor, Mr. Gantelet? [*He puts his hand on his heart, and looks sentimental.*] Well, when the party goes off to-night, do you manage to get on the footboard behind the Countess's carriage, and tell me all that happens.

Gant. Dat I did intend to do already. My master play de

cocher ; I mount-a behind: I tell you all: you give me oder kiss.

Lett. Devil take me, if I do. Get out, you scaramouch. [*driving him off.*] Take care you don't stumble on the Legion of Honors; don't run against Macbeth's angel! [*Exeunt.*

Scene V.

At Racy's Lodgings.
A room elegantly furnished. Italian vases, marble
busts, statuettes, &c., &c.

RANDOLPH,
running about the room with an Italian greyhound.

Rand. There, Tiz, that 'll do; you put me quite out of breath.

Enter SANZACARLINI.

Sanz. I come unannounced, Mr. Randolph.

Rand. Not the less welcome, signor ; my servant has gone on a business of importance. Pray, be seated. You found me, I hope, without difficulty ?

Sanz. Thank you. Yes, I took the direction from your man. You wished to see me on a matter of importance.

Rand. Why, yes; but really — Be quiet, Tiz — I scarce know how to break it to you.

Sanz. It is a matter then of some delicacy. I am not particular.

Rand. So I have heard you say. And it is on that account I have ventured to send for you. In few words, sir: there is a certain gentlewoman whom certain parties find it necessary to overreach, she having endeavored to overreach them.

Sanz. I understand, sir: what I believe is called, in vulgar English, *Tit for tat:* natural equity.

Rand. You have heard, doubtless, of Animal Magnetism

Sanz. As I have of a thousand other bubbles which men blow up one after another, and believe they are solid, though they have made them, themselves, of soap and water.

Rand. Then you have no faith in it.[54]

Sanz. I cannot have faith in that which is founded on what I have no faith in.

Rand. And that?

Sanz. The immateriality of the soul. I believe my senses; but I have no faith in the invisible, the inaudible, the impalpable, what I cannot taste, and what I cannot smell.

Rand. Then you have no belief in your own thoughts?

Sanz. In their permanency, no; in their existence, yes. Where they come from, I know not; where they go to, I care as little.

Rand. Yet they are invisible, inaudible, impalpable; you taste them not, neither can you smell them.

Sanz. [*hesitating, but showing no confusion.*] But Mr. Randolph did not send for me to dispute on metaphysics.

Rand. Hardly: it was a digression of your own making. I knew beforehand, that, with all your intelligence, your shrewdness, your vast knowledge of mankind, you lay no claim to the possession of a soul, nor will allow any other man to have one.

Sanz. [*with the same coldness.*] What convinces Mr. Randolph that he has one?

Rand. That which should make you feel it, who were born an Italian.

Sanz. And what is that? Seeing my country in bondage to foreign tyrants, and its native masters but the overseers, the whippers-in of the miserable, half-starved, ignorant slaves?

Rand. No, no.

Sanz. [*still, in appearance, cold and calm, and speaking in the same grave tone, but with rather more quickness.*] Superstition then? the yoke of a priesthood, who are worse, if possible, than they were, in the days when the great John Boccacci made them the sink of every vice, as you call it, or the personification of every passion, as I would say, — of every dirty passion, that controls this beautiful nature which the world calls human? the paganism of the old time under a new name, and its pollutions no more public? the last link, the rivet, of the chain of mental servitude? Is it this, that should? ——

Rand. [*impatiently.*] No, no! *Dio buono!* you will not listen.

Sanz. [*still imperturbably.*] O, perhaps then, it is the monuments of past *greatness*, as men call it, which have come down to us, a vile posterity, to demonstrate, that as now Italia is but the subject, so once she was the tyrant of nations, that in

other times she swept together, from all parts of the depopu-
lated and wasted earth, the means of embellishing her scanty
corner, and that the gold, the ivory, and the marble, that de-
corated the very baths of her emperors, were transmutations
from the bones and flesh of myriads of their fellow-creatures,
and the milk in which an imperial wanton steeped her cor-
rupting body was the drainings, the conversion of the essence,
of their blood.   Or is it these toys [*pointing to the vases, &c.*],
the reproductions of her ancient genius, the ten-thousand-
times-repeated certificates of her greatest dishonor, " il disdoro
di noverare avi famosi", *the dishonor of counting famous an-
cestors?* Soul? Soul? An *Italian* have a soul? You have
lost your recollection in America.

Rand. No, sir; but you have exploded, and shot so far into
the clouds that you cannot wonder if I am a little bewildered.
Who the devil expected to fire such a rocket by such a *boute-
feu* as I applied to it! *Cristo benedetto!* I was alluding to
music.

Sanz. Music! You really make me laugh. [*without moving
a muscle of his face.*] Music! [*caressing his long mustaches.*]

Rand. Yes, sir. I say, that if I did not have a thousand
other proofs, what I feel here [*striking his heart.*], and the
moisture that gathers in my eyes —— But I talk to an infi-
del ; and with that cold unaccommodating humor of yours
there is no reasoning. Let us drop the subject. [*gravely.*

Sanz. [*Bowing sarcastically, but without smiling.*] Yes, one
cannot long carry a dead weight, and keep floating in the
clouds

Enter Racy.

Rand. Uncle! *À la bonne heure.* You come to remind me of our business. This, uncle, is the Signor Sanzacarlini.

Racy. Am pleased to see you, sir. Be seated. — Ah, my little Tiz! [*Taking the dog on his lap and caressing it.*] Mr. Randolph has informed you, I presume ——

Sanz. But little as yet, sir.[55]

Rand. Your own fault. You would go off in a tangent — to prove you had a soul, while affecting to disbelieve it.

Sanz. I have reached my secant : pray dismiss the problem. This *gentlewoman ?*

Rand. [*Recovering himself at once.*] Well, this gentlewoman I alluded to has, through this notion of magnetism, persuaded a man of property and a father, that he has so close affinity with her that their natures must mingle. It is our wish to undeceive him.

Racy. And, for that purpose, we desire to introduce a rival to her good graces, that shall cut him out.

Sanz. Is the lady amorous ?

Racy. Faith! I don't know. — There, go ; [*setting the dog down.*]— She has made love to two men at once ; and a third might easily bear her off, that should propose boldly.

Sanz. I see. You would not have me marry her ?

Racy. Not unless you are particularly fond of old mutton.

Sanz. My teeth are tender, sir. Has the sheep a golden fleece ?

Racy. No ; but he who shears her for us will find the wool profitable.

Sanz. I understand. I am at your service.

Rand. But you must commence the attack at once.

Racy. And carry the fort by assault.

Sanz. If not impregnable, and you furnish the fascines and ladders.

Rand. The place is weak, and I have already made a practicable breach for you, I imagine. Here comes the engineer.

Enter GANTELET.

Well, what from the enemy?

Gant. Mon Dieu, monsieur, she is one de most Christian enemy dat I haav ever see: she hold up bot cheek; she die wid impationce for to saw *Monsieur le Comte*, and sigh like de vind to be made an *officier* of de *légion d'honneur*.

Rand. [*to Racy*] The result of the letter I took the liberty to send in the Count's behalf.

Racy. Ha, ha! know all about that. Gant., leave us. [*Exit. Gant.*] *Signôr Cóntè*, the breach is open; are you ready to mount?

Sanz. An officer of the Legion of Honor should be always ready. [*Bowing to Randolph.*

Racy. Come, you mistake my nephew, sir. That addition to the title was to render the billet more effective, I dare say.

Rand. Nothing more: a lodgement on the crest of the covered-way.

Racy. Without which, his breaching-batteries could not have been constructed.

Sanz. I never get angry, gentlemen; least of all with my employers.

Racy. And now, signor, as a soldier never fights better than when he is well provisioned, will you permit me the —— [*Taking out his pocketbook and speaking in an embarrassed manner.*

Sanz. Sir, a truce to ceremony. I have come hither with the hope of selling you my services. I find they are wanted. They are my commodity: if you bid me fairly for it, it is yours.

Racy. Then, as a fair dealer, I offer you this note of a hundred dollars. It is for what we have already received, and shall receive, on the invoice. When the goods are fully delivered, you shall have another of the same amount.

Sanz. You are a liberal purchaser, sir: I trust we shall often have dealings together. [*Puts the note deliberately in his purse.*] You see, I have not the scruples of other men, as doubtless [*looking steadily at Rand.*] Mr. Randolph has already informed you. What I do, I do not shut my eyes in doing. I look upon all mankind as governed by one principle, which, though called by a thousand convenient names, is yet the same; self-interest. Your soldier sells his blood, your statesman his policy, your merchant his cotton, and your priest his exhortations: I sell my talents. Those who pay for them, as you have done, shall find me true to the bargain. What can any man more? But you will say that theirs are honorable employments, and, if you should speak what is now passing in your minds, you would call mine dishonorable. Yet you have employed me, and if the work is not fit to be done, yours is

an equal impropriety.   But are not thousands doing daily, in
your republic, things that are many times more exceptionable
than this act of mine? You see men selling their conscience to
party, and their honor to office.   These would be their terms;
honor, conscience: yet they would scorn to say that they have
violated them.   I openly barter my abilities, and I do not
fear to call the exchange a traffic.   If passion, or ambition,
buys *them*, they have their price; mine is money, which is
my necessity.   What else, sir, am I to do for this sum? In
plain words.

Racy. You will go to a house that will be shown to you,
and ask to see a Mrs. Dulruse, the housekeeper.   You will
persuade her, in your own way, to run off with you, at ——
What time did you order the carriages? [*To Rand.*

Rand. At half-past nine. [*Touches a silver bell on the table.*

Enter GANTELET.

Gant. Monsieur.

Rand. How came you to know the signature of that letter?
Answer, sir.

Gant. Pardon, monsieur.   Me and Laytie — de door vaas
demi-ouverte.

Rand. Never do so again.   Now take this gentleman to Mr.
Clairvoir's, and, on the way, tell him all that was in the letter,
and every thing else you know of this business. Then return to me.

Gant. Oui, monsieur.

Racy. You will return, signor, and sup with us.   We shall
sit down in half an hour.

Sanz. With pleasure. A woman that has a will is soon persuaded. [*Bowing, Exit followed by Gant.*

Racy. Confound it, Frank, you have a bad acquaintance there.

Rand. I told you so : but he is one that will never intrude himself. If you wanted to fight, and could not summon courage, he would do your business for you, murder his man, take his pay, and you would hear no more of him, till your next occasion. Is all right at the Upper House ?

Racy. Yes, but we had like to have an explosion before the match was lighted. Dulruse, it seems, has had a fancy for Letty, — no sneaking one either; and lo, just as we were all in train in the front parlor, we heard an amorous scuffle, and Letty rolls in stern foremost through the folding-doors, with the blackguard fastened to her bowsprit.

Rand. *Védi combinazióne !* [56] — How did Mary bear this?

Racy. O, I jumped upon the accidental firebrand, and put it out. We made the struggle pass off as mere earnestness on the innamorato's part and ill-nature upon Letty's.

Rand. And Mary is a creature of such good faith herself, that she believes anything you tell her.

Racy. Ay, she 's a jewel, eh, Frank ! But that villain, Letty, confessed to me she backed her hull into the room on purpose. So I let her into our plot, lest she should spoil sport; and the jade, in return, told me all about the letter. *Adorable angel !* You 're a rare one.

Rand. Ay, fruit of your own grafting. [*Romping with the greyhound.*] Well, nunc', that incident of the foldingdoors will not be amiss, when we come to let Mary know the truth about it.[57]

Racy. True, we can add it to the other evidence; or you can do that yourself, at the proper moment.

Rand. In the coach? Perhaps so. But how are the operations to be conducted?

Racy. O, both the coaches, you say, are to be here at half past nine. Walton must take one, and carry off Kate before we let Dulruse know of it. That will prevent collision and explosion. Then we all start. You take the box with coachy — Take care Dul does not see you, though.

Rand. Never fear. I've my disguise all ready.

Racy. — And off we drive to Hal's. There the Count and I are to see Bub magnetise the widow, till it is time to start. While that foolery is going on, Letty will manage to detain Mary Mildmay, and Dulruse must kick his heels in the street, or in the carriage as he chooses.

Rand. And I on the box. Don't keep us too long, though; or the devil might tempt me to horsewhip the gentleman for pastime.

Racy. Take care of that, you hound. If you open before your time, I'll hang you up by the heels. —Gantelet is to watch at the library door (he has taken lessons in peeping,) and when he sees I'm ready, he telegraphs Letty. Down she goes with Mary, wrapped in a thick veil: off starts the Count with Mother Dulruse; I hold fast to brother Hal — if I shall be able for laughing; and the rest I leave to you and Providence.

Rand. Ha, ha!

Sings.] " Veuves et demoiselles,
　　　　　Dans vos peines cruelles,
　　　　　Venez à moi, mes belles ; " —

I told you so,—

Sings.] "Obliger est si doux!" [56]

But where 's Walton?

Racy. He? Off to the parson's; and Dulruse stayed to gabble with his mamma. But they 'll both be here. I 'll fetch Schuyler myself; for I must post back again to Hal's —

Rand. To see that Letty understands her part.

Racy. What, what! jackanapes. She needs no prompting, I assure you. [*Going.*

Rand. [*Singing.*

"Venez à moi, mes belles;
Obliger " —

[*Exit Racy, shaking his cane at him. The dog flies at Racy, barking.*

Ha, ha! That 's right, Tiz.

Sings.] — est si doux!"

[*Exit Rand. at the other door, the dog following him.*

Act the Fifth

SCENE I. *A room at Racy's lodgings.*
RACY, RANDOLPH, WALTON, SANZACARLINI, and DULRUSE, *around
a table with fruits, ices, wines, &c., lighted by candelabra.*

Enter GANTELET.

GANT. *On demande Monsieur Walton.* [*Exit Gant.*

Racy. [*to Walt., who rises.*] Not going, Schuyler?

Walt. You must excuse me, gentlemen. [*Bows and Exit.*

Racy. [*to Dulr. who looks uneasy and seems inclined to follow.*]
But that is nothing to you, Dulruse. You need not fear; he 'll
not carry off Mary. Besides, our time is not come. Frank,
can't you give us a song?

Rand. With all my heart. Of what sort?

Racy. Jolly of course, and none of your outlandish Italian.
Your pardon, signor. [*To Sanz.*

Rand. [*Starting a bottle of champagne.*] Fill then: I 'll give
you one I made myself.

Dulr. What 's the subject? [*Drinks.*

Rand. Temperance. You 'll take your part, uncle?

Racy. Ay, I 'm of the *Committee.* Gentlemen [*to Sanz. and
Dulr.*] you 're the converts; you 'll sign the pledge?

Rand. That is, join us in the chorus?

Dulr. **Ay,** *teetotal;* all together.   Go ahead.   [*Drinks and fills.*

Song.

Rand. To the brim! to the brim!   Let the bead sparkle high,
    While your voices keep chorus, and eye answers eye.
    Give the pledge.
        Racy.   Not to water.
                Rand. No; drink me, each man,
  Confusion to Matthew, and Charles Delavan!

  All.   Drink, drink?   Ay, drink! hip! drink, while we can,
   .Confusion to Matthew, and Charles Delavan!

Rand. By the goblet of water pale Reason may sit;
Racy. But Mirth grasps the winecup, — Mirth, Fancy, and Wit.
Rand. Bright trio, we pledge ye!
        Both. And, as we began,
  Confusion to Matthew, and Charles Delavan!

  All.   Pledge, pledge?   Ay, pledge! hip! pledge, while we can,
  Confusion to Matthew, and Charles Delavan!

Rand. Love — *Water* and Love?   Ha, ha, ha!   Fy, no more!
    Good night, Mother Reason:
        Racy.   And welcome, bright four!
Rand. Roar in volleys their names;
        Racy. And, no flash in the pan,
  Confusion to Matthew, and Charles Delavan! .

  All.   Roar, roar?   Ay, roar! hip! roar, while we can,
  Confusion to Matthew, and Charles Delavan![59]

Racy. [*Whose voice has been loudest in the chorus.*] "Hip! roar while we can — Confusion to Matthew and Charles Delavan!" [*singing.*]   A fair song, and a jolly, Frank.

Dulr. [*speaking thick.*]   Most delicious; and a deused fine sentiment. [*Drinks.*

Rand. [*Ironically.*]   No body can dispute that.

Racy.   I can.   It 's a deused coarse sentiment.   Bad there, altogether.

Dulr.   I maintain the contrary; [*Striking his fist on the table.*] and he that speaks up for water is a cursed canter, and a white-livered fool.

Sanz.   Come, come, sir; you are wrong.   You don't mean to quarrel here?

Dulr.   *You* wont prevent me, will you?

Racy. ⎱ Fy, fy, gentlemen! no jarring.
Rand. ⎰ *Colle buone, signori, colle buone.*[60]

Enter GANTELET.

Gant.   De *fiacre* — de carrïaage haas come, gentlemens. [*All rise.*

Rand. [*aside to Racy.*]   In good time: I 'm afraid Dulruse has got too much.

Racy. [*aside to Rand.*]   Yes, he may be too brutal.

Rand. [*aside to Racy.*]   If he be, he shall pay for it.   [*Aloud.*]   Another glass, Count?   Another glass, Mr. Dulruse?

Sanz. ⎱ Thank you.
Dulr. ⎰ No more.

Rand.   Uncle, you 're not taking the Count with you?

Racy. Going to introduce him to Clairvoir: there 's sport forward; magnetism.　Good night.

Rand. [*to Racy.*] *Sans adieu.*　Good night, gentlemen. Take care of the steps, uncle. [*following him to the door. Exeunt Racy, Sanz., and Dulr., latter two bowing.*] *Orsù, alle mani:* [61] Gant., you rascal, where 's the coat?　*Vite, vîte donc!* [*Exit* GANT. *by the other door.　Randolph pulls off his coat, singing :*

"Brulant d'amour, et partant pour la guerre," —

Re-enter GANTELET, *carrying a coarse overcoat and a tarpaulin hat.　Continuing to sing, as Gant. helps him with the overcoat :*

"Un troubadour, ennemi du chagrin,
Dans son délire," [*puts on the tarpaulin.*
"à sa jeune bergère," [*draws the collar up over the lower part of his face.*
"Allait partout, en chantant son refrain":　—

Now, Gant., see that Coachy don't start without me, while I take the back stairs.　*Prenez garde.*

Singing.]　"Mon bras à ma patrie," —

Gant.　Oui, monsieur.　[Exeunt, — Rand. still singing :

"Mon cœur à mon amie," — [*and his voice is heard behind the scene :*
"Mourir gaîement pour la gloire et l'amour,
C'est le devoir d'un vail'——[62] [*Voice dies off in the distance, and Scene closes.*

Scene II.

The housekeeper's rooms at Clairvoir's, as in Act III. Sc. I.

Mrs. Dulruse, *dressed off preposterously, and like
a bride, with white roses in her head, and
rouged to the eyes, attitudinizing
before a pier glass.*

Mrs. D. [*curtsying.*]   Countess Sansyleeny, Orficer of a
legion of honors. [*Curtsying.*]   Good day, your ladyship.
[*Curtsying.*]   How well your ladyship looks this morning;
charming!   [*Simpering.*]   Oh sir! you flatter.   Ha! really
[*fanning herself affectedly.*]— my dear Countess — you have
such a glow of health! [*curtsying.*]

Enter Letty.

Lett. And so you have, ma'am : you look like Tisiphone.
Mrs. D. And who was she, Letty ? a countess ?
Lett. No, your ladyship ; but one of the three Graces I read
about in the Classical Dictionary.   She has her head all filled
with roses just like you, and very red cheeks.
Mrs. D. And does Pipsiffery wear such a dress, Letty
dear ?

Lett. No, I am sorry to say, ma'am, that the Graces are re-presented naked, as they live in a warm climate ; but she has a fan in her hand. Is n't that dress too tight for you, my lady ?

Mrs. D. Rather, Letty: it was made in the year 1810, [63] when I was married to Mr. Dulruse, poor dear man ; but I have left the back open, as you see : a shawl 'll hide that.

Lett. And my lord won't want to look at your back, ma'am.

Mrs. D. No ; and I thought it was better to put on this than a common muslin, as I had n't time to get a proper dress made.

Lett. Your ladyship is perfectly right. That short waist is so becoming ! But when is the Count coming, ma'am ?

Mrs. D. O very soon, Letty. [*Playing bashfully with her fan.*] I wanted you here, to tell you what he said to me.

Lett. But your ladyship must make haste ; for Miss Catharine will be wanting me.

Mrs. D. Lor', do you know, Letty, I begin to think it won't do for my boy to stoop so low as Kate Clairvoir. I think he might make a more intelligible match among the mobility in Europe.

Lett. No doubt, Countess ; but then —

Mrs. D. Countess! Lor', don't be so free, child. [*Going before the glass.*

Lett. Pardon, your ladyship. — But then, Mr. Walton is already gone off.

Mrs. D. With that poor little Mildmay. I suppose so. [*Attitudinizing in the glass.*] But my Arnold must n't follow with Kate, I think.

Lett. Well, I don't know, madam ; but, if I was your lady-

ship, I would let him go along with me, just for the fun of
it; and you can stop the match, you know, when you please.

Mrs. D. Yes, and it would mortify the purseproud hussy so,
to find herself not good enough for the man she turned up her
nose at. It 'll be delightful. But, Letty, I must tell you
what the Count said. Said he, falling on his knees, just in this
here way — I 'll show you how: sit down in that chair.
Now. [*Tucking up her dress, and kneeling, in her petticoats, at
Letty's feet.*

Lett. What, my lady! did he pull up his petticoats?

Mrs. D. Psha, you foolish child; what should he wear them
for? is n't he a man? I only do it, not to dirty my dress. —
He kneeled so, and, taking my hand, said he, "Charming
64 Pisseréa!" —

Enter CLAIRVOIR.

Mrs. D., being before Letty, does not see him.

Lett. Pisserea, ma'am! who was she?

Mrs. D. Another of the Graces, surely. "Charming Pisserea!" —

Clair. [*Coming forward*] The devil! madam, are you acting tragedy? [*Mrs. D. rises in confusion, still keeping her frock
gathered up in her hands.*] And dressed off in this extraordinary way! What does all this mean?

Mrs. D. I — I was showing Pisserea — Letty, I mean —
how the Count — how the counts act to their ladies, my
dear.

Clair. And was it necessary to put on this finery, for that
purpose?

Mrs. D. O no! that was to render me agreeable in the Count's — I mean in your eyes, my dear.

Clair. You have greatly mistaken it, madam. But it is time to be in the library; my brother will be here directly. Do throw off some of that stuff; and for God's sake rub off that rouge! [*Exit.*

Mrs. D. To act farce. I shall do no such thing. [*Struts out of the room, still holding up her dress in her hands.*

Lett. [*Falls back into the chair, convulsed with laughter.*] Ha, ha, ha! O! oh! oh! I shall die! [*Goes before the glass, and mimics Mrs. D. in manner as well as words.*] " My dear Countess! you have *such* a glow of health!" — "Lor'! do you know, Letty, I begin to think it won't do for my boy to stoop so low as Kate Clairvoir. I think he might make a more intelligible match among the mobility of Europe." Ha, ha, ha! " He kneeled to me, and, taking my hand, said he, 'Charming Pisserea!'" [*Tucking up her frock, and strutting to the door, like Mrs. D.*] Ha, ha, ha! — O! oh! oh! [*Lets her frock fall.*] Pisserea! Ha, ha, ha! [*Exit.*

    5*

Scene III.

The Library, as in Act I. Sc. II.

Enter Clairvoir. *He sits down. Enter Mrs.* Dulruse.
She takes her seat opposite him, pouting. Clairvoir *stares at
her for some time in silent astonishment :*
Mrs. D. still pouting.

Clair. Really, madam, it is the most extraordinary freak! I
cannot account for such a metamorphosis.

Mrs. D. And I can't see how you can snub a body so. Freaks
and porpoises! Very pretty!

Clair. Porpoises? I never said any such thing. You look,
let me tell you, a devilish deal more like a flounder, belly upwards, with its gills open.

Mrs. D. [*Rising in a rage.*] Flounder! Belly upwards!
I could tear your eyes out! You 're a nasty, fractious, dis-
agreeable, bad-tasteful man, Mr. Clairvoir! that 's what you
are! And I won't stay in your —— O! if I was only sure
that my Count! ——

Clair. If, by your account, you mean your salary, Mrs. Dulruse, you need not let that keep you : I will pay you this moment, [*Taking out his pocketbook.*] and a sum besides that shall

cover any little extra items, and save you the trouble of counting.

Mrs. D. [*Sitting down again.*] Was there ever such a man! [*Affecting to cry.*] I was never — so — treated — in — my — born — days! never, Mr. Clairvoir! Was all our 'finities to come to this?

Clair. But, madam ——

Mrs. D. You never will understand me. Who was talking of pay and salaries? You never had any 'finity, nor affection for me neither, Mr. Clairvoir; no, you had n't.

Clair. [*Softening a little.*] Now you are unjust, madam. Was I to blame for your taking into your head such a monstrous conceit as this? that too on this evening, when ——

Mrs. D. But if I did it to please you, Mr. Clairvoir?

Clair. Why then, my dear, you have mistaken my taste most sadly. [65] If it had been any other evening, I should not have minded it so much; but to-night, when I expect my brother, who is such an unmerciful laugher! — Now do, my dear, be persuaded; go and root up that flowergarden, and wash off your war-paint —— You're too late! devil take it! here 's Frank right upon us.

Enter RACY *and* SANZACARLINI.

Racy. Brother, I have the pleasure to present to you the Count Sanzacarlini. —

Mrs. D. Ah, my lord!

Clair. Eh!

Sanz. [*Making a sign to Mrs. D., and bowing.*] Mrs. Dulruse

and myself have had the pleasure of meeting once before: I
did myself the honor to call to-day at Mr. Clairvoir's when he
was not at home.

Clair. Oh! [*Sanz. again makes signs to Mrs. D. to be quiet.*

Racy. I have brought the Count, brother, to be a witness of
your experiments. If you can make him a believer, you will
do more than the Gospel — [*Aside to Sanz.*] and I 'll forswear
my five senses for ever afterwards.

Clair. If the Count wants faith, I must despair: for this
wondrous science is one of those demonstrations of divine
agency, — of a direct though unaccountable spiritual inter-
action between the sympathetic atoms of beings similarly con-
stituted in their internal and intellectual natures, though differing somewhat in their outward organization, — that do not
appeal to the material and vulgar sense, but to a higher and
immaterial, an ethereal —

Racy. [*Touching Sanz. with his elbow.*] — Supercelestial —

Clair. Yes, almost — tribunal of mental, abstract, and intro-
susceptive cognizance of remote and infinitesimal causalities.

Racy. A most transcendentally diaphanous dilucidation of an
extra-problematical irrationality.

Clair. Brother, I am sure of your jest. But I may convince
you. We 'll proceed to facts.

Racy. With all my heart; and make haste; for we are
pressed for time, and Mrs. Dulruse appears in a similar pre-
dicament.

Clair. In this lady, Count, I have discovered the happiest
disposition I have yet known for the development of these sub-
lime arcana. With your leave, I will proceed to manipulation.

Racy. [*as Clair. puts his fingers to Mrs. D's. forehead.*] Don't let your fingers fall too low, Hal — [*Aside to Sanz., while Clairvoir continues his manipulations*] or he 'll take the color off. Signor, let me congratulate you on the charms of your future Countess; she is the very facsimile of the old gentle-woman of Babylon in the dress of a vestal. What a luscious object! Gods! look at her! a boiled lobster immersed in sillabub.

Sanz. [*aside to Racy.*] You seem to have an appetite. What if I pass her over to you; I am not hungry?

Racy. [*aside to Sanz.*] But she is only to be eaten with bank-sauce. Will you dish her?

Sanz. [*aside to Racy.*] Not with that condiment. How-ever, sir, I shall take her out in a minute; and you may pick what meat you choose, white, red, or green; or I 'll give you the whole, claws and all, if you 'll do without the dressing.

Racy. [*aside to Sanz.*] You are generous; but I should go to such a monster with long teeth; for I fear there is nothing of *the lady* in her head.

Clair. It 's done, gentlemen. Look at that woman: she is now in that state, which, should I not will it otherwise, would be eternal.

Racy. Lord! don't disturb her, Hal.

Clair. Brother! —Yet, from that state, the expression of a wish shall rouse her into complete physical ability. "That state, that state, gentlemen, is the perfection of humanity. Hitherto, philosophers have supposed that man, made in the likeness of his Maker, needed his senses to minister unto his mind; that his immortal faculties were knit up with his mortal, and that their separation could take place only on the dissolution of the body; that, as in his waking moments he sees but with his eyes, feels but with his hands, smells but with his nose, tastes but with his mouth, and hears but with his ears, that therefore, when these corporeal agents were locked up in slumber, the faculties which they put in exercise must be locked up also. Absurd prejudice! relic of a barbarous age! I, I will show you, gentlemen, that man may see as well from the top of his head as from the middle of it; that his soul can wander from his body as well in his lifetime as after death; and that the mind has no need whatever of the senses to teach it the distinctions set on matter. The ethereal molecules of this microcosm, my immortal mind, being under the domination of my will, pass at its direction, as its plenipotentiaries, among the molecules of Mrs. Dulruse's microcosm, mix with them, incorporate with them, communicate and receive intelligence, and by this reciprocal introsusception the double intellect becomes as one, yet remains distinct, is itself yet is not itself, another yet the self-same thing.

Racy. Exactly: as the letter A may visit with plenary powers the letter H, and, mixing with it, make Ah! or Ha! yet A is still itself, and H is still itself, yet neither is itself, but itself is the other self, and the two selves make a single self, which is to each other's self as each other's self is to itself, — which is the ratiocination of an exclamation.

Clair. Francis Racy, facts shall convince you. What shall that lady answer? Where shall her mind wander at my suggestion and command? Be it in Madagascar or in the Hebrides, in the sun or in the moon, in Heaven or in Hell, it is all one.

Racy. No doubt; but I shall be more modest. Let the lady's microcosm be commanded by your plenipotentiary molecules to tell me where Schuyler Walton is now, and what he is doing.

Clair. Dorothy, I have willed you to hear: answer my brother.

Mrs. D. At the altar of a church, and has just passed the ring on Miss Mildmay's finger.

Racy. Ha, ha, ha!· No doubt.

Clair. The devil he has! Are you sure?

Mrs. D. Why need you ask? Or what need you care?

Clair. True; it 's a good match.

Racy. And where is Miss Clairvoir?

Mrs. D. Waiting to marry Arnold; which she will do this very evening.

Clair. Ah!

Racy. Ha! There are our letters magnetised. — Why, brother, the lady is wide awake.

Clair. Incredulous man! Try her. Not, if you should tear every hair from her head, would you force her to open her eyes.

Racy. No, for her scalp has no feeling for its adopted offspring. But let the Count try her; he has a charm worth two of that. [*Sanz. whispers Mrs. D. She opens her eyes, and springs up.*

Racy. [*seizing Clairvoir's arm.*] There! I told you.

Mrs. D. My lord, I 'm yours.

Sanz. [*Mimicking, but with perfect gravity.*] Gentlemen, I 'm yours. [*Exeunt Sanz. and Mrs. D.*

Racy. Why, Bub, you 're speechless.

Clair. [*Struggling.*] Let me go!

Racy. [*Holding him.*] What for? Don't let your microcosm get topsy-turvy, or we shall have another deluge.

Clair. Damn it! have I been bamboozled?

Racy. Now you talk sensibly: no molecules in that at all.

Clair. The viper!

Racy. Pshaw! only a lobster. What now?

Enter LETTY, *out of breath.*

Lett. O gentlemen, O Mr. Racy, here are Mr. Walton and Miss Catharine come back; and I really don't believe they 're married after all!

Clair. What 's all this? Frank, let go of me: I am not mad; but you 'll drive me so.

Racy. There then. [*unhanding him.*] Where are they, Letty?

Lett. In the parlor, sir.

Racy. We 'll be there in a minute. [*Exit Letty.*] Come, Hal; all 's as well as it can be. Let us go see Kate and Schuyler. I 'll explain all on the way; and you shall laugh as heartily as anybody.

Clair. The! ——

Racy [*Clapping his hand on his mouth.*] No bad words. "Look at that woman! She is now in a state" —— Ha, ha, ha! How beautifully her microcosm took in the Count's molecules! "My lord, I 'm yours." *Artful Dodger!* Then the Count: [*Bowing gravely to the house.*] "Gentlemen, I 'm yours." [*Exeunt Clair and Racy.*

Scene IV.

The Drawingroom as in Act I. Scene I.

Walton *and* Catharine.

Enter Letty.

Lett. Such a scene, Miss Catharine! Excuse me, but I should die if I did not laugh.

Cath. Why, what 's the matter?

Lett. Oh, the Count has walked off with the Legion of Honors, and Mr. Racy is —— ha, ha, ha! — Excuse me, ma'am — I never saw such a burlesque in my life. Had you seen the Countess hanging on the arm of her gallant *Orficer*, but begging him to let her " only get a shawl ", and the gravity with which he marched her to the door, *whispering soft, yet nothing fearing,* — ha, ha, ha! Forgive me; I must laugh or suffocate.

Walt. The plot I told you of, Catharine. Your father is, by this time, himself again, I am sure.

Enter Racy *and* Clairvoir.

Clair. [*Taking Cath.'s hand.*] So, Kate, Walton has got you in spite of me. Well, I 'm glad of it.

Cath. No, sir, I am still a spinster.

Racy. Then your web is longer than I thought it, that is all.

Clair. How is this?

Racy. Got into a snarl, I suppose. A plot is seldom wove without one.

Walt. No, sir, the thread is as clear as need be. Ask Miss Clairvoir.

Cath. The truth is, papa,— Schuyler would not have me.

Clair. The devil he would not! Sir! Why, this beats magnetism.

Cath. — Without your consent, sir.

Racy. Was ever such a scrupulous ass! [*Shaking Walton's hand, heartily.*] Run away with a girl, and then not have her! Why, Hal, do you hear?

Walt. It was not my fault, sir : Catharine is to blame.

Cath. No, papa; Schuyler was to blame.

Clair. Come, come; no more mystifications: let them vanish with Mother Dulruse. Mr. Walton, how is this? Speak plainly.

Walt. Catharine, sir, was too good a daughter, as she has always been, to take that, without your consent, which, though you had once given it, it was your pleasure lately to revoke.

Racy. [*Turning aside and wiping his eyes.*] Deuce take such comments on the decalogue!

Clair. [*to Cath.*] Is that true?

Cath. Yes, sir; but Schuyler might have persuaded me to have him, if he had chosen; but he proposed to me to turn back.

Clair. [*to Walt.*] Is that true?

Walt. I cannot deny it : but it was only after Catharine had opened her heart to me, and showed me what was too beauti- ful and bright to spoil.

Racy. [*Wiping his eyes again.*] Curse your poetry !

Clair. But you did then ?

Cath. He did, father ! I should never have been so good a daughter but for him.

Clair. Then he shall keep you so still. Here. [*Taking Wal- ton's hand and joining Cath.'s with it.*] Schuyler Walton, [*speaking thick with emotion.*] you are — the noblest of men that I have ever known — and Catharine — is the most vir- tuous of women. A momentary error made me lose sight of your joint merits; but, from this time, they shall never be out of my sight, nor of that of each other. To-morrow morn- ing, Walton, you shall marry her ; and the fifty thousand which she has from her mother I will make a hundred.

Racy. [*Dashing his hands across his eyes, and rushing up to them.*] Hurrah! [*Throws his arms around all three, and hugs them together.*

Enter at this instant,

RANDOLPH, *in his coachman's coat, but without the hat,* MARY, *and* SANZACARLINI ; GANTELET *following.*

Lett. Lord! will nobody hug me ?

Gant. [*Running up to her, and endeavoring to embrace her.*] *Oui, ma chère ;* I vill.

Lett. [*Recoiling. He stumbles, and falls upon the floor.*] Manners !

Rand. [*To Racy, as the group now breaks.*] Ha! old Ursa Major! strangling the whole company?

Racy. Hold your tongue, Canis Minor: they 've almost strangled me with delight. I 've made three of the happiest people in the world, Frank, that were, before, the best, and all by my plot.

Rand. Which is not yet over. Here are three more of the pieces.

Racy. That 's true! Eh! what have you done with the two others? Signor, where 's your Countess? Mary, where 's your groom? How came you all back so soon? Speak!

Clair. } Ay, let us hear it! [*Cath. takes Mary by the hand,*
Walt. } Come, Frank. *and places her beside her.*

Racy. Form a semicircle, good people. So. Now, Mr. Spokesman.

Rand. There are two: put the Signor at the other horn of the crescent. Well: [68] so soon as Miss Mildmay appeared, Dulruse took her out of Letty's hand, placed her very civilly in the carriage, and jumped in himself. Scarcely had he got seated, before the Signor squeezed the Countess on the front seat, and sprung in after her. Gantelet put up the steps as quick as lightning, and, before Arnold had quite recovered from his surprise, the carriage was off at a rattling rate up Broadway. Then began the war. I had taken care to have the window next the driver's box down; and I could hear Dulruse, for a moment, storming like a devil, roaring to the driver to stop, and ordering the intruders out. Suddenly there was a calm, the Signor having said something that effectually laid the tempest. On we drove, — the driver, treble-feed, lashing his horses very much to my satisfaction, — shot by Union-place, and turned up the old Bloomingdale road, when, all at once, there was another hurricane. I could hear now distinctly, as we moved over the softer ground, Arnold make love to Miss Mildmay for cousin Catharine, adjuring her to forgive him, pleading passion, etc. etc., — then Mary, who had at first been speechless with surprise, discovering his mistake, — then Dulruse swear, — then Miss Mildmay burst into tears, then faintly scream (for her brutal partner, it seems, shook her violently,) then Dulruse swear again, and the Signor sternly order him to be silent and to behave himself. Dulruse now sprang up in the carriage, Mary — Miss Mildmay crying all the while, and ordered us with a horrid oath to stop. So we did. *Animo, signore;* it is now your turn.

Sanz. The carriage stopped, Mr. Dulruse forced open the door, and told the young lady to get out, or he would fling her out. [*Here the company use various exclamations of horror and disgust.*] Before I could interfere, Mr. Randolph had sprung down, seized him by the collar, hurled him into a puddle of mud and water that was in the road, and taken his place in the carriage. It would have been a pity, ladies and gentlemen, to separate mother and son, so I tenderly placed the Countess beside him [*the company smile*]; and we drove back, and left them.

Racy. *Alone in their glory.* Ha, ha, ha! But how did the old lady take this specimen of pious consideration?

Sanz. Not like a lamb. You see, she has torn the ribbon from my buttonhole.

Racy. And made herself, without you, an *Orficer of a legion of honors.* [*the company, with exception of* Sanz., *laugh.*] Signor, the merchandise is delivered : here is the balance of the account, with my thanks for the good order in which I have received it, and my acknowledgment that it corresponds exactly with the invoice.

Sanz. [*Depositing, with his customary gravity, the note in his purse.*] We are now, sir, quits. Let me say I have never performed any obligation so much to my satisfaction ; [69] and I feel a sensation, almost of pleasure, here [*putting his hand to his heart.*], that I never thought I was capable of enjoying. If this is a good action, and I should have the good fortune to perform many more, I may come in time to believe in conscience, and have respect for my fellow-creatures. As a proof of my sincerity, I would ask permission of this company to see the end of so pleasing a drama.

Racy. With all our hearts. [*The rest bow.*] And it is coming soon enough : look there !

Enter
ARNOLD DULRUSE *and Mrs.* DULRUSE ;
*the latter with her dress disordered, torn, and
spotted with dirt, her roses drooping, and her rouge
in streaks ; the former, without his hat, and covered, from head
to foot, with mud. Both in a rage.*
MARY, *in terror, takes* RANDOLPH *by the sleeve of his
coat, and presses close to him.*

Dulr. [*To Racy.*] Mr. Racy ! —
Mrs. D. [*To Sanz.*] You villain ! —
Dulr. [*To Mrs. D., stamping passionately.*] Madam, will you

be silent?   Sir, [*to Racy.*] what the devil do you mean by this dirty trick?   It is of your contriving, I know; that jacka-napes, your nephew, would not have brains for it.

Rand. [*Shrugging his shoulders.*]   *Che scioc'co insolen'te!* [70]

Racy. As for the trick, sir, that is your own; and it has been a dirty one, I see. [*pointing to Dulr.'s clothes.*]   I hope you have no bones broken?

Dulr. [*Striding up to Rand.*] For you, sir! ——

Rand. [*Gently shaking off Mary, and going close to Dulr. Sings.*]   "Tu—— E tant' osi?   [*with affected energy.*]   Va, spergiuro!" [71]
[*with affected scorn.*

[*The company laugh, with the exception of Sanz., who looks on coldly.*]

Dulr. [*to Rand.*]   Coxcomb!   [*To the rest.*] You are very pleasant, ladies and gentlemen.   [*smiling with affected sarcasm.*]

Rand. [*to Dulr.   Singing.*

> " Deh ! non voler costringere
> A finta gioja il viso :
> Bella è la tua mestizia
> Siccome il tuo sorriso." [72]

Racy. }
Clair. }   Ha, ha, ha !

[*Walt. and Cath. smile.   Mary looks frightened, and Sanz. cold.   Letty and Gant. enjoy the scene in a suppressed manner, at a distance, and mocking Mrs. D., who stands fixed, with a ludicrous expression of mingled rage, irresolution, and fear.*]

Dulr. [*Furiously, — shaking his fist at Rand.*]   Puppy !

Rand. Come, come, this is going too far. [*Taking him aside and speaking in a lower key.*] You know where to find me, if you please, to-morrow. Leave the house, now, before you make me forget where you are, — as you have forgotten it, yourself, too much.

Sanz. [*To Rand., and drawing Dulr. from him.*] Pardon. Allow me, Mr. Randolph. [*Bowing to the rest.*] Will the company permit me? [*Leads Dulr. to the front of the stage, — Dulr. following reluctantly and uneasily, yet angrily.*] Mr. Randolph has given you a hint, I presume. Do you mean to call him out?

Dulr. What business is that of yours?

Sanz. [*With same coldness.*] This much. Perhaps you do not know what is known to every gentleman in this city, — that Mr. Randolph is the first shot in the country: that he fences like a master, I can assure you from my own experience; and the vigor of his arm you have felt too recently to have forgotten. [*Dulr. shows signs of impatience.*] Be very quiet, sir; you had better. — If you meet Mr. Randolph, and survive it, that same hour you shall have to do with me. If you will inquire of Mr. Randolph's servant, he will tell you that he has seen me, on shipboard, repeatedly split his master's bullet, and disarm him twice when we played with foils; and *I* tell you, I do not value the life of a man a fig: if you escape him, therefore, you die by my hand. No words, sir. [*sternly, yet coldly.*] Go, and disgrace yourself and this house no more.

Dulr. [*In a subdued, but sullen tone. To Mrs. D.*] Come, madam.

Mrs. D. [*To Clair.*] I suppose, you 'll let me have my clothes, you old fool!

Dulr. [*stamping violently.*] Will you be silent?

Clair. [*To Mrs. D.*] Send for them when you please, with what is owing to you.

Lett. I 'll hand them to your ladyship [*curtsying.*] when your ladyship pleases. [*curtsying.*

Cath. [*severely.*] Letty!

·Mrs. D. [*Shaking her fist, in a rage, at Lett.*] Hussy!

Dulr. [*Dragging Mrs. D. off.*] Will you come, I say, woman? [*Exeunt D. and Mrs. D.*

Rand. [*As they retreat, and with his eyes upon them. Singing with affected melancholy and bitterness.*

> " Pasci il guardo, e appaga l'alma,
>   Dell' eccesso de' miei mali;
>   Il più tristo de' mortali
>   Sono, o cruda, e il son per te." [73]

Clair. So ends my folly as *The Magnetiser.* But I do not regret it; for it has made me the proudest of fathers. [*Looking at Cath. affectionately.*

Cath. Me, the happiest of daughters. [*Returning the look.*

Walt. And me, both the happiest and the proudest of husbands. [*Pressing Cath.'s hand.*

Racy. — That is to be. And it has saved an angel from a hell upon earth. You do not repent it, do you, Mary?

Mary. [*Pressing Racy's hands affectionately, then smiling.*] My preserver!

Racy. No, not quite; don't you make love to me, you puss: there he is. [*Pointing to Rand. Mary blushes, and casts down her eyes.*] Did you explain the little interlude of the drawing-room, Frank?

Rand. Yes, uncle; in the coach. Did you not tell me to?

- *Racy.* Ah, rogue! you have used your time well in the coach, I suspect. [*Looking with satisfaction at Mary, who grows still more confused.*

Rand. So well, uncle, that with Mary's permission, and your approbation, I mean to devote as much more as possible to the same employment.

Racy. Mine, you dog? You know it is my dearest wish. Take Lim, Mary, and ninety thousand dollars which I give you with him.

Rand. Uncle, I will cut off these curls, and present them to you to-morrow, with my *moustache.*

Racy. Will you? That insures you ten thousand more. And what will you do with your d—d opera-tunes?

Rand. I will not sell them, lest I should strip you naked. I will teach them to Mary; and she shall sing them for me, with such an angel's voice, they will be damned no longer.

Racy. [*His eyes moistening with delight.*] That 's my boy! Is n't he a pretty fellow, Mary, when he talks sense? Once off with his coxcombry, and I 'll match him with any other he in the Union. You rascal! [*pulling him affectionately by his long hair.*] marry her soon, [*Lowering his voice a little.*]¹⁴ and get your old uncle a boy. What will you call him?

Rand. [*aloud and mischievously.*] But is it to be a boy? It may be a girl, uncle.

Racy. Rot your girl! Don't plague me, Frank. What will you call him?

Rand. Francis Racy, uncle.

Racy. Will you? [*seizing his hand.*]   But — suppose there should be twins?

Rand. Then I 'll call them both, *Francis:* Francis the First, and Francis the Second.

Racy. Hurrah! Gods! are there no more people to be made happy?

Lett. [*Coming forward with Gant. by the hand; she curtsying, he bowing.*] Yes, if you please, sir. I have taken it into my head to civilize this French frog; and, if you like to encourage the Home Mission ——

Racy. What then?·

Gant. Why then, sare, ve vill do our best posseeble to raise you up a leetel *communauté* of Christians. [*Letty pinches his ear.*] *Ouf!*

Racy. Ha, ha, ha! so I will. I will make a collection for you, my pious couple.

Clair. Walt. Rand. ⎞
⎟ We 'll all contribute.
  Cath. & Mary. ⎠

                              [*Letty curtsies,
                    Gant. bows, with his hand on his breast.*

Sanz. Nothing so likely to render them zealous in the discharge of their functions.

Rand. [*To Racy.*] Still another pair, old Hymen!

> *Singing.*] " Unisco le famiglie,
>   Le liti io rendo nulle,
>   E spesso alle fanciulle
>   Marito soglio dar." [75]

Racy. At your opera snatches, again, puppy ? Is this your promise ?

Rand. To-morrow, you know, to-morrow : we 're through the catastrophe, but our play is not yet done.

Racy. We 'll stop it then immediately ; for the actors have performed enough for one night.

Clair. [*smiling and taking Racy's hand.*] But the audience, I trust, has too much *affinity* to be tired.

Curtain falls.

NOTES

NOTES TO THE MAGNETISER

1.—P. 5. *Come along, there's a dear!* etc.] For the Stage, omit to the close of the paragraph, and, previously, "through the blinds."

2.—P. 7. *Letty saw them,* etc.] Omit this sentence; also the last, commencing, "Come, Mary darling."

3.—P. 10. *He is quite unworthy,* etc.] Omit to the close of the paragraph.

4.—P. 10. *Fy! what scrupulosity!* etc.] Omit to "*Cath.* Well then, since you are so delicate."

5.—P. 10. *I will speak for you,* etc.] Omit to "You think her, Schuyler"— on p. 11.

6.—P. 12. —*the more so,* etc.] Omit this clause.

7.—P. 12. —*where the experiments,* etc.] Omit to —"and before I knew"— 7th line below. The Stage cares nothing for these moralities.

8.—P. 13. *Besides, my dear Schuyler,* etc.] Omit this sentence. Then, changing *Now, have you a desire,* etc. to " Now, I want you to observe this folly," omit again down to " *Walt.* But how will your father, etc." 11th line below.

9.—P. 13. *But first,* etc.] Omit to —"nothing that is not dishonorable," on the next page.

10.—P. 14. *Where now are,* etc. etc.] Recite instead : " Where now the primordial bounds set by Nature to human action and to human thought ? "

11.—P. 14. *Man, no longer a creature,* etc.] Recite : "Man no longer shall say unto the worm, Thou art, *etc.*"

12.—P. 15. ' — *sees now,* etc. etc.] This is one of those *ad captandum* passages which are meant to vary with the date and place of the performance. Local and temporal allusions become, in a different locality and at a different epoch, pithless, if not partially unintelligible. The reading therefore has varied with various occasions on which I had hoped for the performance of *The Magnetiser.* For example. in 1860, it stood : — "now scents the issue of the Italian struggle, now tramps before the General in San Juan [the issue of the China [Russian] war, now tramps before the Colonel in Mosquitia], now prognosticates the sex of the forthcoming progeny of Eugenie, *etc.*"

And for this reason, I restore the original one, which would have been more than intelligible at the time of its composition, in February, 1842. To-day, recite : —"sees now the issue of the Cuban struggle, now prognosticates the settlement of the *Alabama* question ; and the tardy conveyance and uncertain news of steamships and telegraphs are entirely superseded."

13.—P. 17. — "on silks.] To-day : —"on crinoline."

14.—P. 17. — *of the genus* Homo.] After this insert, for the present year: "Do you see any horses? *Mrs. D.* No, but a sight of velocipedes; some with two wheels, some with four, and — I do declare! there goes one like lightning, with a little wheel besides, like a knife-grinder's, only it is at bottom instead of atop. *Clair.* They must have a genius for mechanics. And do they ride these stall-less steeds head downward? *Mrs. D.* Yes, and move the treddles with their hands. *Clair.* While their toes ply the steering-bar! Head downward! Why, it is a moral photograph of what goes on with us below! The moon perhaps is a caricatura of our earth; or a real limbo of vanity. Are you tired, *etc.*" — But the whole of this talk promotes in nowise the action, has in fact nothing to do with it. It is therefore contrary to my own rules of writing. Omit then from "*Mrs. D.* O yes, there goes a man," on p. 16, to "Are you tired", p. 17, — throwing out previously, on p. 15, "I want to know what the people there are doing."

15.—P. 18. — *John Jacob* —] To-day: — "William B." —

16.—P. 18. *Do not ask me.*] Omit to "His name begins with A." Or, throw out all between "much happier," at foot of p. 17, to "It is —" on p. 18.

17.—P. 20. — *get our children by magnetic conjunction* —] Omit.

18.—P. 21. — *evil* —] The Stage can omit this epithet, if it likes.

19.—P. 22. — *Townshend, Hartshorne, all of them.*] As originally written, "Townshend, Hartshorne, Stone." These were writers, expounders or witnesses of the absurd doctrine or its imagined illustrations, that were in vogue in 1842. The lapse of time has deprived the subject itself of part of its zest. Seven and twenty years

6*

ago, Animal Magnetism, revived in the New World, was in its glory in Manhattan, and had drawn into its fanciful superstition as many educated persons as the still greater frenzy of spiritualism does now. Both are bubbles which break not by the breath of the comic and satiric writer, but by coming in contact with some newer and larger bubble, which in its turn will float in the atmosphere of public favor, till broken in like manner or resolved into nothing by the mere fragility of its existence.

20.—P. 23. *He, I see plainly*, etc.] Omit to " The disrespectful ! "— 5th line below.

21.—P. 23. —*my congenial spirit*, etc.] This allusion to the government's " Fiscal agents " would in that day have *brought down the house*. There is no young person that would now understand it. Next, the passage read: " *Clair.* —" no ideality ! no prospective ratiocination ! no sense but the dull stale sense of precedents. . . *Mrs. D.* —" That for your Hyder-Alities ! that for your respected rotten Austrian nation ! that for your blood-stained French Presidents ! " Allusions, which would have taken happily enough some twenty years ago.

For to-day, recite : " *Clair.* Time enough for that, my congenial spirit ! — Mere corporality ! no sense but that dull stale sense the body ministers, or of staler precedents. [*Exit*, etc.] *Mrs. D.* Time enough, you old fool, you ? Let me, *etc.* That for your Geneva spirits ! that for your pauperalities ! that for your toady Ministers and tailor Presidents ! "

22.—P. 25. *D—nation !*] The Stage can substitute, if it choose, " Perdition ! " But the exclamation in the text is the one that would be used, under the circumstances, by the character, who, I beg to premise, in view of Act II. Sc. I. (where, consistently with his general turpitude, he is made to appear as a bad and impious son,) must be sometimes coarse in his violent and unrestrained impulses. *Dulruse* was meant to be totally without self-control, blasphemous, licentious, treacherous. This for the closet, that is, for the reading of literary men. In acting, however, the case is different, and his vehemence and virulence may, as in the present instance, be toned down to suit the requirements of the Theatre.

23.—P. 29. St. John's Square.] This locality, like the allusions noticed in Act I., is of course alterable according to the occasions and proprieties of the time. *St. John's*, or *Hudson, Square* was in 1842 a fashionable neighborhood. At the present day, we should read *Union Square.* Some year or two hence, even this will be unsuitable; and the time is not far distant, when, if the *Magnetiser* should be performed, the meeting between Walton and others of the Scene must occur outside the *Central Park.*

24.—P. 31. *He and the housekeeper*, etc.] Omit to —"he sees me on the stairs."

25.—P. 33. Lett. *O sir, don't flatter me*, etc.] Omit to "When Mr. Dulruse had done " —

26.—P. 35. — *old woman* —] See, above, note 22.

27.—P. 36. — *clout* —] — "bib " — if the Stage elect.

28.—P. 37. — *I have it*, etc.] Omit to "You shall let Miss Clairvoir " — on p. 38.

29.—P. 38. — *personate her lover, without talking* —] Omit this clause; also, "or anybody else," in the next line.

30.—P. 41. Mrs. D. *Do let me*, etc.] Omit to "*Mrs. D.* O Lord ! *etc.*" ten lines.

31.—P. 41. — *which my Arn* —] Omit to the end of the sentence. Then, in the next sentence, omit between the two semicolons.

32.—P. 45. "*Allons, enfans*, etc."] The commencement of the Marseilles Hymn :—

> *Rise, children of the fatherland !*
> *The glorious day at length has come* — :

33.—P. 46. "*Amici*, etc."] From Rossini's opera ; *Il Conte Orÿ :* the opening of the *cavatina :*

> " Amici, il Ciel pietoso
>   Le vostre preci accolga,
>   Un rio destin non tolga
>   La pace a voi del cor."

> *Friends, may a Heaven of mercy*
> *To your prayerful requests give reception,*
> *Nor ill fortune nor cruel deception*
> *The peace of your hearts take away.*

34.—P. 47. — *on* mi sol !] Pronounce full, as *soul :* the quibble, of these two notes of music, being in fact for *my soul.*

35.—P. 48. Che questione curiosa !] *What an odd question !* Below : "Poter di socco !" an untranslatable Tuscan exclamation, meaning literally *Power of* [the] *sock !* as if we should swear *By the Muse of Comedy !* Pronounce : *Kay quays-ts-o'na coo-re-o'sah !* and *Po-tair'.*

Fanny Ellsler, Taglioni, Rubini are of a past day. Recite therefore the whole passage thus :

"*Rucy.* What, what ! You lie, you lie. But what detained you in Philadelphia? The new opera-dancer?

Rand. The new — opera - dancer ! *Che questione curiosa !* She

never shows her legs, you know, till evening. And then, have I
not seen the ancles of the best in Paris? *Poter di socco!* you
might as well tell me of some second-rate tenor of the Academy,
when I have been rapt into the seventh heaven of ecstasy on the
breath of the foremost at the *Italiens.*"

As to the expression in the text, — "of Bergamo," I should observe perhaps, that I was told by an Italian composer that the tenors
of the opera have almost all come from that place : a curious fact, if
it is one; and as such he regarded it himself. Rubini was, I think,
a native of Bergamo.

36.—P. 49. — his long curled hair —] This was the fashion
of the day. Omit, now, " *long.*"

37.—P. 49. "Deh! ti calma!"] *Ah! calm thyself* [be calm].
From *La Sonnambula: Atto 2°*.

38.—P. 49. — *and Delilize your locks*, etc. etc.] Recite at
present: "and Delilize your whiskers, to stuff her chignon.
Rand. [*still*, &c.] A "rat" were better, uncle. *Racy.* Confound
you, sir! is this the fruit of your three years' tour in Europe?
You left us, a fellow of some sense : what, &c."

39.—P. 49. Ella mi va lusingando:] *You flatter me.* And below: "zio mio", *uncle.*

40.—P. 50. — *fearing that*, etc.] Omit this clause.

41.—P. 51. "Unisco le famiglie, *ec.*"] From the *Conte Orÿ:*
the *cavatina*, as at the commencement of the Scene :—

> *I unite again friends that are sever'd,*
> *Their bitter contentions I soften,*
> *And to the young damsels often*
> *A husband am wonted to give.*

42.—P. 51.   E come!]   *How could it be otherwise?   How can you ask?*   The Stage may substitute "How else?"

43.—P. 52.   Avete sempre furia!]   *You are always in such hot haste!*   Pronounce: *Avay'ta sem'pra foo'reah.*

44.—P. 53.   — *has been an officer of Napoleon's* —   To-day: —"has served with the French at Magenta."

45.—P. 54.   — *Palmo's* —]   To-day · —"Taylor's."

46.—P. 54.   — *Windust's* —]   To-day: —"Delmonico's."

47.—P. 55.   — his hair short —]   To-day: —"short whiskers."

48.—P. 55.   "In me ciascun si può fidar."]   *In me everybody may confide.*   A continuation of the arietta above: —

> *And to the young damsels often*
> *A husband am wonted to give.*
> *All men may in me believe.*

49.—P. 56.   SCENE II.]   For brevity's sake, this entire Scene may be omitted.

50.—P. 57.   *I've been,* etc.]   Recite: "I was very unhappy, while I thought," *etc.*

51.—P. 64.   — *Broadway.*]   To-day: —"Fifth Avenue."

52.—P. 64.   — *enjoy you.*]   For the Stage, —"possess you."

53.—P. 65.   *And being younger,* etc.]   Omit, in recitation, this clause.

54.—P. 68. *Then you have no faith in it.*] After this, omit to the Entry of Racy, on p. 70: "Uncle, *à la bonne heure.*" The greater part of what is thus included, namely, commencing with the words "I knew beforehand" (p. 59,) was never meant to be recited. But, more fortunate than my comedy, Italy has improved in the long interval, and the sarcastic description put into the mouth of one of her children has happily ceased to be even an outline portrait.

55.—P. 71. *But little as yet, sir.*] After this, omit to "*This gentlewoman?*" and, throwing out the stage-direction (*Recovering himself at once.*) make Randolph's part read, "Has persuaded a man, etc.," excluding the clauses previous.

56.—P. 75. Vedi combinazione !] *There's a scrape ! — What a dilemma ! — What a jumble !* Some such phrase. Literally: *Behold combination* [of circumstances.] Pronounce: *Vay'de cohm-be-natz-e-o'na.*

57.—P. 75. — *the truth about it*] After this, omit to "But how are the operations to be conducted ? " then all after that to —"the Count and I "— in Racy's part.

58.—P. 77. "Veuves et demoiselles, *etc.*"] The French paraphrase of "Taccia di tanti mali, *ec.*" in the *cavatina* of the *Conte Orÿ*, before cited:

> *Widows and bashful young maidens,*
> *In the sweet troubles that grieve you,*
> *Come unto me ; to relieve you*
> *Is always of duties most dear.*

59.—P. 79. *Confusion to Matthew and Charles Delavan !*] Although Father Matthew is not forgotten, yet the name of the zealous and persistent advocate of temperance in this country, before the advent of its "Apostle," will hardly convey an impression to the present generation. Substitute therefore, for *Charles Delavan,* "all of that clan"; which is an insipidity, and clumsy, but intelligible.

60.—P. 80. Colle buone, signori, colle buone.] *Soft words, gentlemen, soft words.*

61.—P. 81. Orsù, alle mani:] *Now for action.*

62.—P. 81. "Brulant d' amour, *etc.*"] The commencement of a well-known French ballad: —

> *Burning with love, and parting for the war,*
> *A troubadour, a foe to sorrow's pain,*
> *In the wild love he to his fair one bore*
> *Went everywhere thus singing his refrain :*
> > *My arm for native land,*
> > *My heart at love's command ;*
> *Gaily for them both to fight and death endure*
> *Is the duty of a valiant troubadour.*

The actor may give but a verse or two of the stanza, at his option.

63.—P. 83. —1810—] To-day: — "1850."

64.—P. 84. — *Pisserea !*] Recite: —"Cisserea ! "

65.—P. 87. *If it had been,* etc.] Omit to — *to-night :* which read "To-night too"— Then omit, below, "be persuaded."

66.—P. 89. *That state —*] From here, may (at the discretion of the Theatre) be omitted down to the last sentence: "The ethereal molecules, etc."

67.—P. 96. — *Well :*] After this word, read the paragraph as follows: "Scarcely were Miss Mildmay and Dulruse seated in the carriage, before the Signor squeezed his Countess on the front seat, and sprung in after her; and away we went at a rattling rate up the Avenue. Then began the war. I could hear Dulruse, *etc. etc.* On we drove, shot by Union-place, and turned up the old Blooming-dale road, when, all at once, there was another hurricane. Dulruse, discovering his mistake, sprang up, *etc. etc.*"

68.—P. 97. Animo, signore:] *Come, sir.*

69.—P. 98. — *and I feel* —] Omit, to " As a proof of my sincerity."

70.—P. 99. Che sciocco insolente !] *What an insolent blockhead !* Pronounce: *shocco.*

71.—P. 99. "Tu —— E tant' osi ? *ec.*"] From the *Sonnambula, Atto* 2°. (changing the gender :) —

    Thou —— And thus dar'st thou ? Go, thou perjur'd !

72.—P. 99. "Deh! non voler, *ec.*"] From *Anna Bolena, Atto* 1°:

    Ah ! seek not with feign'd joy to hide
    That brow's expressive sadness;
    Beautiful is thy sorrow's frown
    As is thy smile of gladness.

73.—P. 101. "Pascl il guardo, *ec.*"] From *La Sonnambula, Atto* 2°.:

    Feed thy looks, and let thy spirit
    With the excess of my ills be sated;
    The saddest of all men created
    Am I, O cruel, and am for thee.

74.—P. 102. —*and get your old uncle*, etc. etc.] Substitute : — "and make me a grand-uncle. What will you call your boy ? "

75.—P. 103. "Unisco le famiglie, *ec.*"] See Note 41.

THE PRODIGAL

OR

A VICE AND VIRTUE

MDCCCXLV

CHARACTERS, Etc.

STOCKTON, *a rich India merchant.*

STAUNTON, *a wealthy Englishman, also an India merchant.*

BUZZ PICKINS, *an English author of note, on a tour in America.*

REVISE PROOFSHEET, *an "enterprising" publisher.*

HEILIGER SCHURK, *Stockton's bookkeeper, a German by birth.*

ARTHUR, *Stockton's son.*

HENRY LEDGER, *Stockton's second clerk.*

JOHN DOUGHTY, *an American, confidential servant to Staunton.*

HANS GUTERKNECHT, *a German, servant to Stockton.*

MRS. STOCKTON.

THERESA, *Arthur's wife.*

CLARA, *Arthur's sister.*

Two BURGLARS; *a German* TAVERNKEEPER;
FRANCIS, *a shopboy;* PETER, *servant in Stockton's household.*

SCENE. *Philadelphia.*

TIME. *That occupied by the action.*

THE PRODIGAL

OR

A VICE AND VIRTUE [1]

ACT THE FIRST

SCENE I. *A parlor in Stockton's house.*

STOCKTON, *in a high passion, dragging
himself into the room with difficulty, owing to the efforts
of his wife, who is clinging to him, while he endeavors to
loose her hands and shake her off.*

Stock. Speak no more! not a word! not one syllable! I tell
you, for the thousandth time, my resolution is fixed; and, so
help me God! from this moment ——

Mrs. S. [*putting her hand over his mouth.*] O no, no, no, no!
not that! for your own sake, Stockton! [2] for your peace of

mind here, and your hopes of peace hereafter, do not swear!
do not! [*sobbing and letting go her hold of Stockton, who for
the moment appears shaken.*]   Think, he is your only son,
our first-born, whose birth we looked for so fondly, Arthur,
when our love — our *love*, do you hear me, Arthur! — was
yet new, whom you called after your own name ——

Stock. That he might disgrace it.   Woman, you do well to
remind me.   Is it the babe, the child, the boy even, the good
and dutiful boy ——

Mrs. S. O yes, remember that; he was always good and
dutiful ——

Stock. [*stamping passionately.*] Will you have done?   Does
not the dutifulness and goodness of his early years make the
disobedience and misconduct of his confirmed manhood more
striking, and more intolerable?   How do I know? perhaps
his docility was fear, pure animal fear of a father that[3] — that
loved him [*with emotion.*] — as only a father, such as I am,
loves an only son that is such as he appeared to be *then.* —
Be quiet, Sarah! — But when he is too old to feel this fear, —
when, I say, he has reached that age that I should have looked
to reap the fruits of the good seed I had planted, what then
does this good and dutiful son?   Ruined by your indulgence
and flatteries ——

Mrs. S. My husband!   Arthur! ——

Stock. I say it, by your and Clara's flatteries.   Will you
deny it?   Did you not encourage in him, you, you two
women, his love of letters, as he would call it; weep at his
tragedy and laugh over his comedy, till the youth believed
himself a new Shakspeare in the drama, and born to supplant

John Milton, or John Milton's devil for aught that I know, in the Pandemonium of epic foolery ——

Mrs. S. But, husband, you took delight yourself in his talents ——

Stock. In his *talents?* Surely; as I did in his manly beauty, and, as I fondly believed them — oh my God! [*striking his forehead.*] what idiots fathers are! — in his virtues. But was it that he might forget everything else for these darling *talents?* was it, I ask you, as the pauper of a garret, the threadbare associate of starveling poets, sneaking painters, and strolling playactors, or as the heir of five millions, the honored companion and ally of princely merchants, the rival of the best of them, and to take the lead of most? Talents! I meant that they should make his fortune, not mar it! Yes, fool, fool, fool that I was, I dreamed — Did you ever have a dream, madam? [*turning abruptly to his wife, who only weeps.*] Well, I was boy enough — yet you see my hairs are gray, quite gray — I was boy enough, this grayhaired man that speaks to you, to dream that by these very talents, and by that fortune, the name of Arthur Stockton might be a watchword of true, of rational liberty, in the citadel of the nation; nay, perhaps I went further in my waking visions, and saw his honored head —— Derision! curses and derision! [*walking up and down, impetuously.*]

Mrs. S. And why should it be a dream?

Stock. Why? Sarah, are you turned a fool? quite a fool? [*taking her hand, with a cold gravity, and looking in her face, while she manifests fright.*] Did you ever hear, woman [*fiercely.*] of a *poet*, a moneyless one at least, in the senate of a nation?

of a painter guiding with his twopenny maulstick the destinies
of a great people? [*with increasing passion.*] of a damned mer-
ryandrew of a playactor signing vetoes in the seat of Washington? — With money indeed [*bitterly and ironically.*] it
might be feasible, for we are getting, like wiser nations, to
make a merchandise of our country's interests, and a million
votes would cost but little more in our land than in our grand-
dame's; but I have cut him off — I have and will! — with a
single shilling, with the half of a shilling.   Begone! [*waving
her off.*

Mrs. S. Mercy!   You will not be so obdurate!   Mr. Stockton — husband — Arthur; they will starve, they ——

Stock. [*with new fury.*] *They?*   It is well reminded.[4]
[*Bitterly.*] Ha, ha! *they!*   This is another fruit of talent,
and of association with talented people and paupers.   But for
this, this marriage.— this accursed buckling with a nameless
brat ——

Mrs. S. O no! don't say so! don't abuse her: she is our
daughter's friend.

Stock. Not the less nameless, not the less a brat for all that.
Who was her father?   Was he ever seen or heard of?   Did
not this Mrs. Ellison,[5] with her thin, melancholy, hypocritical
face come over here all alone, husbandless, all but pennyless,
from England, with her little child, and was there ever word
said of its father — by her at least?   She had good reasons
doubtless; for, when others asked about him, she would blush
and tremble, or look pale and haughty, but never answer a
syllable.   Then comes the school-intimacy of the brat Theresa
and our little Clara ——

Mrs. S. You never opposed it, Mr. Stockton; you — you [*hesitating.*] seemed to encourage it.

Stock. Don't interrupt me. So I did. What would you have? I was not quite a brute:[6] and the good manners of the little girl, her beauty perhaps — malediction on it! — made me forget the distance fortune had placed between her and Clara; indeed I was proud, like an ass that I was, to think that Clara should have no pride. —

Mrs. S. Like a Christian, like an angel that you were, say.

Stock. [*stamping impatiently.*] Again! Like an *ass*, I say, that I was. Yet how was I to foresee the consequences? or did I, because I looked with pleasure on the childish attachment of two little schoolgirls, suppose that it was to increase with their growth, expand into a vigorous friendship, and twine its abominable limbs about the brother also? But when I did, did I not endeavor to prevent it? did I not? Answer me that!

Mrs. S. Alas!

Stock. [*with bitter mockery.*] *Alas!* You cannot answer: [7] you know that I not only did all I could to break up this ill-omened attachment between the boy and girl — which I suspect that you and Clara privily encouraged — don't interrupt me! — if you are innocent of the charge, so much the better for your conscience — I not only did that, but I absolutely forbid his further association with her, when he had arrived to puberty; and when afterwards I discovered, too late, that their friendship had grown to love, and that Arthur made his very poetry and pencil minister to the flames of his passion, did I not gravely take him to task as a father should, unfold to him,

as if he was a friend and equal, my expectations, and show
him the impossibility of fulfilling them, unless he broke off all
connection with a person, for him so dangerous ? What did
he reply ? What, this dutiful, this good son, this man of talent
answer to his father, and his sober and friendly adviser? Answer me now ; — what, I ask you, did your poet, your play-
writing, player-consorting son, the companion of drunken
artists and lewd opera-singers, what did that pretty gentleman — what did the villain answer ? [*shaking her by the
arm.*

Mrs. S. Oh, Mr. Stockton!

Stock. [*with a cynical smile.*] Oh no, he did not answer that,
not quite that, Sarah Stockton : he told me [*flinging her arm
off.*], me, his father : " That till now it had been an honor as a
pleasure to obey me" — you know he was always a dutiful
boy — " but that honor was superior to filial duty, and that
plighted affection no parent had a right to violate." So much
for Milton and the devil! Did he not talk like a Roman ?
[*with bitter energy, and a sardonic smile.*] Was he not worthy,
this honorable and unbending young man, to be dreamed of as
a successor of Washington ?

Mrs. S. O my husband ! why repeat all this, when I know
it so well ? why aggravate ——

Stock. Because I wish to impress it upon your memory, [8] —
not in fear that you may have more sons — thank God, we
are past that! but lest Clara should be tempted to imitate her
pattern of a brother [*Mrs. S. seems ready to sink, from confusion.*], and I may have two children [*looking sharply into her
face.*] to turn out of doors, instead of one.

Mrs. S. O God help us both! you are wild with passion.

Stock. Am I? You shall see that my memory at least is sane, and that I can reason well for the future. I answered him, this good and dutiful and talented son, I answered him [*raising his voice almost to a scream or yell*]: " Then marry — and make your bridal-bed in a garret; for the day that you do so, Arthur Stockton, you are no son of mine. Go!" And he did go — I helped him from the room with my arm — and he did marry! he did [*with the same terrible vehemence of tone.*] — he married — he, the heir of millions and my only son, and namesake, my hope [*with emotion.*], he married a girl without a cent, and without a name. [*recovering his energy and passion.*] He did, curse ——

Mrs. S. [*eagerly, placing her hand again before his mouth.*] O no, don't curse him! remember, Stockton, he is our son, our only son! oh, oh, oh! [*weeping.*

Stock. Well, I will not *curse* him. But, from this day,' that I have first learned the extremity of his folly and his ingrati-tude — an ingratitude he did not dare with all his effrontery, to make known to me himself — I cast him off forever! There [*significantly.*], tell that to Clara — as a lesson. [*He is about to rush out from the scene, when*

Enter, CLARA.

Mrs. S. O Clara! your father —

Stock. [*looking back.*] Has just confirmed his sentence against the Prodigal; nor are you the governor that shall re-prieve him, let me tell you, whatever your sympathy with evil-doers. You are the child however that may yet be able to take a lesson. Teach it to her, madam. [*Exit.* *Re-enters directly.*] I shall not return to the office. Let some one be sent to Mr. Ledger, to tell him that I want to see him immediately. Don't make a mistake, Miss Stockton, and go yourself. [*Exit.*

Mrs. S. [*throwing herself on Clara's neck.*] O Clara! my son! your poor brother!

Clara. Mother, do not despond! papa's nature is too good to suffer him to keep this mind long; and then Arthur's character is so exalted; there is so much in him to love and to admire!

[10] *Mrs. S.* Ah, my dear; there is the danger: parents naturally expect more from good children than from bad; and, where they have almost everything as they wish, to be disappointed in one or two things comes with a greater shock than a hundred crosses where they look for nothing else. Arthur's disobedience is the one spot upon the sun —

Clara. That will soon have passed, and leave us once more happy in its warm and beautiful beams.

Mrs. S. You are always looking at the bright side of events, Clara.

Clara. And wisely, mother; for thus I have always some share of light; while you, with that dear, sad brow forever toward the dark, are constantly in the shadow of either anticipated or actual evil. Yet I could be gloomy too, just now; not merely for Arthur's sake, but for my own. What was that "lesson"? what meant that allusion to Mr. Ledger?

Mrs. S. O my Clara, I fear I have been criminal where I

thought only to be just, and have unintentionally encouraged attachments that may end in depriving me of both my children.

Clara. Never, mother! even if one be lost to you — which I do not believe.   Whatever my feelings, I certainly shall not prepare myself for the duties of a wife by becoming a disobedient daughter.

Mrs. S. My good Clara! so like your brother! yet without his self-dependence, and too lofty pride of character.   But —— Mercy! what is that? [*A crashing noise within, as of furniture smashed,* [11] *mixed with a sound as of the violent and sudden vibration of the strings of some musical instrument; then a window is heard to be thrown up violently.*

Enter Hans.

He has a small cabinet-picture in his hand, and his looks evince great perturbation.

Hans. O madam! Miss Clara! *mein Gott!* de mashter has broken every ting in Mr. Artur's shtudy!   For dis twenty year I haave nefer seen him in so mushe passio'n.

Clara. The pictures! the pictures! speak, Hans.

Hans. Gone.   I did n't get in de room till Mr. Shtockton haadt jumped on de beautiful new piano, ant was smashing him in widt his feet as if it vas one paltry oldt bench, and I saw de two pictures Mr. Artur value so much,[12] vich just come from de great shale of de Cardinal Fish in Italy, and stoodt upon de floor, one kicked clean out of de frame and de oter wit a big ole in his middle, and de floor all trodt ofer wit blatters of paints, and broken brushes out of Mr. Artur's box.

Mr. Shtockton nefer looksh at me, he seem so blindt, and shpringing off de piano, throwsh up de vinder, and fling out bot' de guitar. Vile he do dis, I take de chance, snatch de little pictur vich Mr. Artur paint himself two year ago from Miss Theresè, and comes here.[13]

Clara. Thanks, thanks. [*taking the picture.*] How fortunate [*to Mrs. S.*]: had he seen this! —

Mrs. S. It had driven him mad. But the books, the papers?

Clara. [*eagerly.*] Yes, yes, my brother's manuscripts?

Hans. [*sadly.*] O I forgot to say, Miss Clara; when Mr. Shtockton jump from de piano before he seize de guitars, he caught up from a table de book dat Mr. Artur was reading from lasht night —

Clara. His comedy, his new comedy!

Hans. Yes, dat please Mr. Ledger so mush, — and crying out in a vay dat make me feels badt, fery badt, Miss Clara, "Talents!" flings it right into de fire. [*Clara wrings her hands.*] But dere 's de bell: the ladies perhaps vould not vish to see nobody?

Mrs. S. No, no; bid the porter make our excuses. And, stay, send somebody to the countinghouse; Mr. Stockton desires to see Mr. Ledger immediately.

Hans. Yes, madam. [*Exit.*

Clara. What a misfortune! an hour longer, and Arthur would have had all the little furniture he needs, sent him.[14] His manuscript too, his play — that he had just finished! I could almost cry.

Mrs. S. And those paintings, that cost him so much money! perhaps ruined forever.

Clara. Yet I think, mother, that this little picture saved will make him forget all the rest.

Mrs. S. True.   But make haste and conceal it. [*Exit Clara at one side, while on the other*

Re-enter HANS.

What is the matter?

Hans. O madam — it is Mr. Schurk — he has just gone up to de mashter's room.

Mrs. S. Well?

Hans. Yes, but — pardon me, madam — it is n't vell; it ist ill.   If you knew —

Mrs. S. [*gravely, yet mildly.*] If I knew?   You forget your place, Hans, and presume perhaps too much on your long services.   This is the second time to-day, about Mr. Schurk.   If you have anything to tell of him that concerns your master, or us, take it to the master only.

Hans. Ah, but to-day, now! how vould I dare? he vould not listen ——

Mrs. S. Did you send to Mr. Ledger?

Hans. Yes, madam; Peter has gone.   [*Retiring*]   *Mein Gott!* dey are blindt — dey vill not let me open deir eyes.

[*Exit,* —   *Mrs. S. looking after him with surprise;*

and the scene closes.

SCENE II.

*Stockton's private parlor.   In the middle, an oblong
ebony writing-table, with a massive bronze standish.
A letter lying open on the table. —   STOCKTON is seen striding up and down the room in great agitation ; while near
the door, in a respectful attitude, stands
SCHURK, apparently unnoticed.*

Stock. [*muttering* to *himself, by starts.*]   Dreams, dreams,
dreams! — and how miserable has been my waking! —   In-
fatuated!   I should have known what would result. —   But
there shall be no spread of these liberal principles — one pauper marriage shall content even Mrs. Stockton.   But, to lose
all my hopes, all! — [*Raising his head in a sort of despair, he
sees Schurk.*]   Oh, Schurk! my son is gone, my only son, my
Arthur!

Sch.[15] Heaven!   Mr. Arthur dead?   The Lord giveth ——
[*throwing up his eyes.*

Stock. No, no! but lost, — lost to me, lost to society, to the
world.   He is married, sir.

Sch. Oh, well, is that all?   there is nothing — pardon me,
Mr. Stockton — so very extraordinary in all that.

Stock. [*impatiently.*]   But there is though.   He has married a pauper, a nameless —— Read that, sir. [*snatching up the letter, and flinging it to Schurk.*]

Sch. [*taking out from his pocket, with great deliberation, a pair of spectacles, and adjusting them on his nose; then reading slowly, while Stock. seems devoured by impatience.*]

" Sir, — It is my duty to inform you that your son has been married for more than six weeks to the illegitimate daughter of Kate Ellison." Illegitimate? bastard, ha! *das ist ärgerlich.*[16]

Stock. [*stamping.*] Sir! — it is death! How can you be so cold? But go on, go on, sir! [*beating the palms of his hands together.*]

Sch. " This evil is too late to remedy, but the knowledge of it may serve to prevent another of a like kind. It begins to be noticed that Miss Stockton and Mr. Ledger are more tender in their manner to each other than is common between mere friends, or is likely to please you." *Ach, ja!* " The brother's example —— But you need no more; this hint will be enough, and the fact that it comes from one who, though he does not wish to be known in such a matter " — *in der That! man kann Sie wohl glauben* — " is yet religiously bound to communicate it, being one whom you have a thousand times obliged." Stuff! stuff! it is all one lie [*crumpling up the letter, with a show of contemptuous indignation. — Stock. looks at him with surprise.*] Pardon me, my much honored patron, but do you not see this letter is anonymous? The man is afraid to tell his name; he is therefore either liar or coward.

Stock. Coward he may be, [*Sch. winces, twitching his specs.*] but liar he is not. Arthur is married, I have told you already, and married to Theresa Ellison. He acknowledged it this

7*

afternoon; and this afternoon [*with an effort.*] I turned him out of my doors.

Sch. Good God! you don't mean it. Poor Mr. Arthur!

Stock. What, sir, you too! will no one think that I am right? [17] has a father then nothing to expect from his children, but that they should not kick him or pilfer his money? has he no right to demand in return for birth and education and patrimony, that they should not dishonor his name and enrich beggars with his affluence?

Sch. My good patron, and kind master! you know I can have no wish to justify Mr. Arthur for any wickedness,[18] for often have I risked the favor you have honored me with by daring to remonstrate with you on many of Mr. Arthur's little faults and neglects of duty, and revealing to you his bad associations, in hopes that you might reform him [*Stockton shows impatience, and even resentment.*] — pardon me; but for one serious disobedience to take such severe measures! Ah, think how much in the sight of God we are all evil creatures, and that, if we do not forgive in this world ——

Stock. The devil take your piety, if I must say so! do you call this a simple disobedience, to ——

Sch. Serious, Mr. Stockton; I said, serious, very serious.

Stock. Well, serious; don't interrupt me, sir. Is this all then I have to complain of? Did I not, when you first showed me, as you were bound,[19] being in my confidence, and in the important place you hold [*Sch. bows humbly.*], how constantly he neglected his duties, that presumptuous Henry Ledger making up his deficits in secret for him, did I not, when I ascertained the cause to be his *passion* [*bitterly em-*

phasizing the word.] for poetry and the arts, did I not indulge him to his heart's content, only exacting of him to be present two hours every day in the countingroom? Has he not had thousands on thousands to expend upon pictures and pianos, indecent statues, wormeaten books and rusty medals? and when I found he would be nothing but a student, and he had the effrontery to tell me so, did I not forgive him this too, and allow him to withdraw entirely from commercial life? — but not that he should spend his hours in the greenroom and the music-halls, not to be hand and glove with fiddlers and mountebanks, not to be a Prodigal in his misprized genius as well as with his money. No! Yet when I pardoned this too, had I any reason to expect that he would marry without my knowledge, and in the very face of my expressed wishes and intentions? Answer me that, Mr. Heiliger Schurk. You cannot, any more than Mrs. Stockton or Clara can. But even this disappointment, this crushing of all my ambitious hopes as a father, even this I should have felt with less anguish, had the blow come less sudden and rude, had I learned this dishonor in fact from his lips, and not from that letter. Six weeks! who had a right to know that before his father?

Sch. Why, that is true! and who could be so insolent as to inflict this blow on a father. [*opening and smoothing the letter.*] Let me see. Why, this is singular! I never saw any hand so like my own. Look here, Mr. Stockton.

Stock. I cannot see it at all, — not the least resemblance.

Sch. No? that is strange. My very *A's* and *I's*! Mr. Ledger would say so at once.

Stock. Ah, you remind me. I have just sent for him, to show him this very letter.

Sch. [*startled.*] Show it to him? But you don't believe the insinuation: it is a mere calumny — only fit to burn. [*flinging it, as if from an indignant impulse, into the grate.*

Stock. [*snatching it, before it has kindled.*] Why, sir, Mr. Schurk, what do you mean? Ah, pardon me, my old friend; I understand your feelings. But for this letter, it can do no more harm; that is too late; and it may do good. It has proved but too true in one part; why should it not be so in another?

Sch. But how will you discover that, by showing it to Mr. Ledger? He will deny it, true or false.

Stock. No, he will not.[20] You do him wrong, sir. To give the young man his due, he is like my unhappy son, one of the very few men in this world that would not tell a falsehood, though perhaps their life depended on it. It has been one source of the strong friendship between him and Arthur, this very point of honor, and in turn this friendship has nursed their mutual pride and spirit. If Mr. Ledger deny the presumptuousness here charged to him [*striking the letter.*] I shall believe him without further question.

Sch. And if he own it?

Stock. Or do not own it; if he merely refuse to deny it — he shall seek employment elsewhere: I could not bear him any longer in my sight, — though I should lose his services with regret.

Sch. Not with so much regret, perhaps, did you know all.

Stock. Ah! what do you mean to insinuate? But you are no friend of Ledger's, I have seen that long.

Sch. Heaven forbid! I am not the young man's enemy because I do not like his ways.

Stock. But he is regular in his duties.

Sch. Yes, and in his attendance upon theatres and operas. His friends are not such as a young merchant ought to have.

Stock. [*violently.*] The curse of evil communication. You goad me. No matter; he will be here presently, and we shall see.

Sch. [*hastily.*] Well sir, I must hurry home: we have closed later than usual on account of the specie you expected, which has just arrived. In waiting bank-hours to-morrow, I have locked it up in the double safe.

Stock. It is a large amount, Mr. Schurk; but it will be secure there, at least for one night. You could not have done better.

Sch. There are the keys, sir. Good evening, Mr. Stockton. [*going.*] But — pardon me — I should not think it safe to trust too much to Mr. Ledger's honor, in the matter of that letter. We used to say in my country: "Das ist eine schlechte Maus, die nur ein Loch weis": *'T is a sorry mouse that has but one hole to run to.*

Stock. Well, well; be easy; I have a trap to catch him, though he had fifty: he must be an old villain indeed that can look me in the face, and mean such a wrong.

Sch. [*abruptly.*] Good evening, sir. [*Exit.*

Stock. Eh! Everybody seems to be as mad as myself, this evening. This evening — [*dropping into his chair, by the table.*]   Oh, Arthur! Arthur! [*covering his face with his hands.*] my son, my son, Arthur! [*Scene closes.*

Scene III.

Same as Scene I.

Enter Clara.

Clara. [*pensively.*] I must contrive to intercept Henry before he sees my father; there is some mischief brewing. That letter which revealed poor Arthur's marriage — may it not have told another secret ? [21] Papa's insinuation, and threat, which make me blush to think upon, though I have not indeed deserved them — what else could they imply! Yet who could be so wise ? who but my mother, or Theresâ, or at most Arthur, could even suspect what has surely never passed my lips to anybody, and which I have endeavored to keep even these tell-tale eyes from revealing ?   But I must not be down-hearted ; no, nor frightened : either would be something new for Clara Stockton. [*Recovering her full spirits as she speaks, word by word.*] All will yet be well — I am sure of it — I am determined it shall ! — yes, it shall be, with papa, and Arthur, and Henry, and me, and everybody. Yet I would give sixpence now to set my eyes upon the he or she, that could be wicked enough to send such a mischief-making letter.

Enter SCHURK.

Sch. [*aside, delightedly.*] *Welch ein Glück!* [22] — [*Coming forward.*] Miss Stockton, I am delighted to meet you at this moment. —

Clara. [*coldly.*] If you knew what I was wishing, you would scarcely think it such happiness — supposing I had my wish.

Sch. And what was that?

Clara. I was wishing, sir, to see the face of the — the devil —

Sch. Hey!

Clara. — For it could only be such — that could find the heart to send such a letter to my father.

Sch. [*with some confusion.*] As what? Letter?

Clara. Yes, letter. I thought you had just left Mr. Stockton: surely, he showed you a letter?

Sch. O yes, yes: a poor, miserable, cowardly, anonymous bit of stuff, such as I would have thrown into the fire. I did indeed; but your father rescued it.

Clara. No doubt to find out its author, — as he will one of these days. Good evening. [*going.*

Sch. Ah, Miss Stockton, always my foe?

Clara. Always my own friend, Mr. Schurk. If I do not find it particularly agreeable to entertain you, of late, I need not repeat the reason why.

Sch. Ah, Miss Stockton, would you but see with your mother's eyes or your father's! —

Clara. They would be rather old eyes, be it said with reverence; and I should not think that such a medium would be favorable to the views with which it has pleased you of late to honor me: but I see with my own, and they tell me —— [*looking full at him: he casts down his eyes.*] No matter what they tell me. Enough that if you can talk piety with my mother, and commerce with my father, you have not yet learned the subject that most interests their daughter; and so she leaves you. [*Curtsying and going.*

Sch. [*maliciously.*] Perhaps I have; but I do not usually make my calculations for any other *ledger* than my own.

Clara. [*with spirit, and turning full on him.*] For Mr. Stockton's clerk, sir, you give your wit too much margin; nor will you find that such false entries [*he starts, and looks at her suspiciously.*] will count up much to your profit in the journal of my favor. I beg you will leave the room. And, mark! never again touch upon this subject; or I may forget that you are useful — in the countingroom.

Sch. [*quite beside himself.*] When the merchant's daughter lends her eyes to her father's second-clerk, she cannot blame the head-clerk if he puts in a bid for her ears.

Clara. [*a moment confounded, but directly recovering, and drawing herself up with quiet dignity.*] Since *you* will not, sir, *I* go, — never from this day to exchange a word with you again. [*Exit.*

Sch. [*fiercely — between his teeth.*] Go, in the name of all the devils!— It was my last throw there, and it has turned up blank. Remains now but the last desperate one. Should that fail! —— O accursed spirit of gaming! [*Exit.*

Scene IV.

*The hall of the house, leading to the street-door.
The lamp from the ceiling is not yet lighted, and the scene is
demi-obscure, as at the coming-on of
twilight.—* Hans *standing in the passage.—
Enter,* Schurk.

Sch. [*in a soft voice, and looking anxiously about him.*] Hans !
[*Hans endeavors to avoid him.*] *Ey, Hans, lieber !* — *Was ficht
Sie an ?* [23] [*seizing him by the arm.*

Hans. Ve musht spreak English in tis house, *mein Herr.*

Sch. [*looking again on every side of the passage.*] *Wohlan !* [24]
Will you do that ? *Frisch !* quick ! shall I see you —, down
there ? — soon ?

Hans. [*hesitating.*] Yes — perhaps so. Y — es ; I 'll come.

Sch. [*still in a low voice.*] Remember ! five hundred !

Hans. Yes, I 'll see you. [*Exit Schurk.*] But first, I 'll see Mr.
Artur. — Oh, dat my faterlandt should send ofer such men,
to dishgrace her and all honest Germans ! [*Exit.*

Drop falls.

ACT THE SECOND

SCENE I. *A street, with shops and dwellings intermixed. On
the left is seen a bookseller's shop with its appropriate sign,
and showbills of new publications attached to the posts of the
door and frame of the window. The perspective of the
street runs diagonally from corner to corner of the scene,
appearing to wind to the right above, and to turn off to the
left in the foreground. The lamps of the street are lighted,
but not of the shops ; and during the acting of the scene a
shopboy comes out of the bookseller's and takes in the showbills : — which indicates twilight.*

Enter

STAUNTON, *and* DOUGHTY, *looking about them curiously :
Doughty plainly dressed, as a gentleman's
servant out of livery.*

Staun. Well, Jack, here we are ; safe in port, as you would
say.

Dy. Yes sir, snugly moored ; out at present on a pleasure-
excursion in the captain's gig. Which way do you steer, sir ?

Staun. Faith, my boy, I cannot tell you. Everywhere this
is a new country to me, and yet,[25] strange as it may seem, I
am here on one of the most important occasions of my life,
though there is not a single place marked out on my chart to

guide me, save this solitary port of Philadelphia. And now that I am here, I scarcely know where to begin my exploration. The place however is well known to you, I suppose.

Dy. Ay, ay, sir. I have shipped at this port, many 's the time and oft, though I hail from Maine — down-east, as we Yankees say. The last voyage I made, howsomever, was from Bosting.

Staun. When you were wrecked, you mean.

Dy. Ay, sir, in the China seas, when all on board save me were murdered by the dam ——

Staun. [*holding up his finger.*] Jack !

Dy. Pardon, sir. I shall get broke in time. But we Yankees take a kind o' naterally to swearing, ever since the *Blue Laws* went out. —

Staun. "Blue Laws"? what are they? Yet I think I have heard of them too.

Dy. No doubt you must, sir. Why you see, Mr. Staunton, . they were just a set of regulations made by a kind of people, that had very good intentions, but did n't know how to give 'em effect. So they laid a fine on a man for kissing his wife on Sundays, and had him up to the gangway for chewing a quid amidships, and gave him a round dozen for squirting an oath or two it mought be in the eye of the wind; which was about as unseamanlike a manœuvre against the breakers of immorality, as if I were to attempt to clew up the mainsail in a stiff breeze with a bit of common seizing. Them were the *Blue Laws*, Mr. Staunton.

Staun. A Nautical Ephemeris and Practical Navigator compiled by landlubbers and quack astrologers, eh ? I think,

my boy, my forefinger will be quite as effectual to keep you
in the course.

Dy. Yes sir, I shall steer close, I hope; but I shall occasionally need to hear my captain's: *Steady! Nothing off!
Don't shake her!*; for, as I said, swearing comes nateral to
me as a Yankee; and besides, if I fall off a point or two as
yet, I am but a raw hand at the wheel, you know, sir; it's
not a twelve-month since you took me up starvin', and all but
naked, and reproachin' Providence that it had not let me per-
ish with my shipmates, — not knowing that the darkest hour
of my life was but the dirty morning of my breeziest and
fairest-weather day.

Staun. How should you? you are not a barometer. But
come, John Doughty, shut up the logbook. We are both well
quits, I believe; for if I have done you any kindness, have
you not repaid it, you silly dog, by sacrificing for me your
independence?

Dy. Not so much sacrifice after all, sir: for, in the first
place, I'm not so much scared at the name of *servant* as my
countrymen usually are; we're all servants, when obliged to
haul taut and belay at another's bidding; and then, I would
rather be first-officer of such a crack ship as I now sail in,
though her capting is an Englisher, than to be the second-
mate, as I was, of a blas ——

Staun. [*holding up his finger.*] Jack! — And in the third
place [26] — for you've sailed long enough on this tack, and
must now about ship — you are no servant at all, but rather
my traveling companion; an humble one, if you will, but not
less a companion; and one, I trust, to keep with me, until I

can put him into a situation where his true and stout heart shall have a wider and more proper field of action — a better berth, in short. But come, we have been gazing long enough about us. " R. Proofsheet" [*reading the sign on the opposite side of the street.*], "Publisher, Book-Seller and Importer.'' That stationer's will be as good a shop as any for the inquiries I have to make ; and I am partial to the trade. — Hush ! [*putting his hand suddenly on Dy.'s arm, and arresting his movement and his own. They have both for the last few minutes been standing under the windows of a simple dwelling, nearly opposite the book-seller's. Just as they were about to cross the street, a female voice was heard singing softly, approaching nearer and nearer to one of the windows, which was seen open, and is now shut down, cutting off the sound at once.*]

Dy. A sweet pipe, sir.

Staun. Yes ; but the words ! Ah, you do not know. "Ye streams that round my prison creep". . . Strange that the first thing almost to greet me in this strange city should be that simple and too well known air ! [*Musing.*] — I will accept it as an omen ; and a good one it must be. Come on ; there is a man in the shop-door, a jolly-looking fellow too, as if to encourage my search ; cheerly. "Ye streams" —— 'T is very odd. [*As they cross over, Proof., who has his hat on, walks down, and they meet in the foreground.*]

Staun. Pray sir, may I be permitted to trouble you ——

Proof. With pleasure. Excuse me. [*suddenly.*] Good evening, sir, [*to Arthur, who has just come out from the very house where the singing was heard, and, moving down the scene, passes*]

close to the group, bowing mutely to Proof., and Exit to the left.]
Mr. Stockton! [*calling after him.*] Pray, sir! — He is wrapt
up, I suppose, in some new poem, and does not hear me.

Staun. Mr. Stockton, did you say?

Proof. Yes, sir, Mr. Arthur Stockton, one of our most considerable ——

Staun. Arthur! — what! — No, that is impossible; he is
ten years older than myself. A son, probably.

Proof. Yes, son of the old man; only son; has but one
sister; of course, large fortunes, both. The son's a very literary man — a poet, sir, — and painter too, by the by, — has a
play to be performed this very night at the Chestnut.[27]

Staun. [*with evident satisfaction.*] You don't say so? Excuse
me, — but I have a singular predilection for men of genius,
and —— Where does Mr. Stockton reside?

Proof. Can give you his address in a minute, if you'll step
to my place. Indeed I have a parcel —— [*As they move off,*
Re-enter ARTHUR.

Oh, Mr. Stockton, the books you sent for ——

Arth. I have just turned back to ask you about them.
Have they come, did you say? [*Staun. draws back a little, yet*
keeps his eyes on Arth., who does not observe him. Dy. turns
round, and walking off a step or two, looks curiously up at
the house where the voice had been heard.

Proof. Yes, sir. [*Rapidly.*] Boettiger, Bosse, Bottari, Bos-
chini, D'Hancarville, Felibien, Hamilton, Mengs, Millingen,
Millizia, Stuart and Revett, Visconti ——

Arth. [*sadly, not testily.*] O have done, have done, my good
sir. The bill [*anxiously.*] is rather large?

Proof. Would be to some — but to you a mere trifle : some six hundred; 637 dollars, 50 cents; — that is, for the works on painting and antiquities alone.   You know there is the *Etruscan Remains* — 4 volumes, magnificent copy, in perfect order — cost a hundred by itself; and the *Athens*, and the *Herculaneum* —

Arth. [*interrupting him.*] It is much more than I had hoped. However, I came back to tell you, that you are not to send them to my father's, but over the way — there, [*indicating the house he had come out of.*] No. 92.   Good night.   [*Exit, hurriedly.*

Proof. There ?   Why —— And so gloomy !   Sir, [*to Staun.*] I have not now the opportunity I expected; a parcel, or rather a cartload, I was to send to Mr. Stockton's is not to go there —— But stay ! do me the favor to come into my place; I recollect now — there are some books to go to Miss Stockton.   If you will wait till they can be got ready, one of my boys will show you the house at once.

Staun. Really, you are very obliging : I 'll —— Doughty, you may amuse yourself as you please; I shall easily find my way back to the hotel.   [*Going off with Proof.*

Dy. Thank you, sir; I 'll just cruise about here, and keep within hail. [*Saunters slowly up the scene, looking carelessly about him, but throwing a glance up at the window of 92, while Staun. and Proof. enter the shop, and*

Scene closes.

[28] Scene II.

*The publisher's private room, commanding, through
a door in the back of the Scene, a perspective view of the entire
shop, lighted by lamps. The room is surrounded by
shelves having some choice books in costly
bindings. Busts of eminent poets, on pedestals.
A round table with various new books, pamphlets, etc.
upon it, and an astral lamp, which
lights the room.*

*Enter, from the shop, PROOFSHEET, bowing
the way to STAUNTON.*

Proof. Take this chair, sir; [*rolling a heavy, leather-covered,
great chair nearer Staun.*] you will find it more comfortable.

Staun. Thank you. [*Seats himself. Proof. takes a smaller
chair on the other side of the table.*] You are doing me more of
a favor, in more ways perhaps than one, than you can readily
imagine; and I foresee that this, though the first, will not be
the last day of our acquaintance.

Proof. [*bowing very low.*] Sir, I am infinitely indebted —
shall feel honored by your good opinion and custom — all the
new works —— By the by, there are some on this very
table, my own publications. Perhaps you would like ——

Staun. That is not exactly what I meant, though undoubt-
edly I shall be a large customer. [*Proof. again bows.*] And,

by the by, since we speak of it, what volume is this now, with the antique masque on the cover? Something quizzical, I dare say. [*Opening it.*] American, eh?

Proof. Bless you, sir, yes; and by the very gentleman we have just parted with.

Staun. Eh, what! [*delighted.*] Let me see: [*Reading the title.*] "The New Book of Metamorphoses: Cantos 1. and 2." — This by Stockton's son? I must put this at least aside, to take home with me.

Proof. Thank you. Yes, that book is more like what we are accustomed to receive from the Old World than any of its kind that has ever been written in America. Hence, and as it dares to tell the truth, it has made more enemies than perhaps any other book of home-production.

Staun. Ah, I see [*glancing over it.*] : satire. The author sets up for a wit.

Proof. Sets up? No, that is his chief offence — that he does not set up for anything, like everybody else around him. He is in fact a wit: they dare not deny it; so they call him *coarse:* a poet, beyond peradventure; so he has a *knack at rhyming:* a scholar, very evidently; therefore, a mere *pedant:* a man of taste; and consequently, he is *behind the age.* In fine, being liberal, he has got it up in superb style, as you see: so, to give an edge to their insolence, his enemies, — which is, almost all the Philadelphia of little authors and vulgar journalists, proclaim him a rich coxcomb, who has paid me, the worthy publisher, a handsome price to make myself ridiculous; for, as you see, the book is anonymous, and I, the godfather, suffer for its sins.

VOL. V.—8

Staun. It is damned then?

Proof. Most effectually! simply because it is the only book of poems ever published in America, with but few exceptions, that did not deserve to be damned at its birth, and irredeemably. Indeed, sir, Stockton is not even counted among our poets, although no one could be able to prove he is not one of our best. There they are, in that large volume, big and little, poets and poetasters, yet nowhere the author of the *New Metamorphoses*, — not one line!

Staun. You astonish me and pain me.

Proof. Why so? To read Mr. Stockton's books we should be a polished nation, with at least a fair proportion of wits, scholars, and true critics, to the merchants and shopkeepers: and yet we are not. Mr. Stockton is in fact in advance of his age.

Staun. You do not know what delight you give me. Is there anything else of this young man's writing?

Proof. Yes, half a dozen volumes of novels, and sundry plays and poems.

Staun. You shall put them all up for me. But what was their fate?

Proof. The same bottomless pit. All damned, sir, — just as easily as heretics were formerly roasted, and are now — in flames typical, — for the mere fact that they durst follow principle instead of fashion, and worship the true divinity of nature and beauty, instead of worthless idols made up of wood and red rags.

Staun. Why, you almost give the lie to your own condemnation of the incompetence of your countrymen. [*Proof.*

bows.] You have quite excited me. Did you not say a play is to be performed this evening, of this poet Stockton's?

Proof. Yes, "the Last Farquharson"; a tragedy. They are to attempt it; but it has been rejected by every theatre in the country save Burton's. Burton has had more discernment; though I fear there will be a packed house of hissers and groaners.

Staun. Shame! shame!

Proof. No sir, it is right. Did I not say, he is a wit? What right has he to be so, when there is no wit in the country? It is un-national, sir, unpatriotic, aristocratic in fact. Were he to perpetrate the Punchinello buffoonery of the Slicks and Suggses, or even the Tom-of-Bedlam extravagance of the Carlylists, — the low, miscalled "Yankee", slang, seasoned with blasphemy and redolent of scoundrelism, which is christened "humor" in a thousand books and papers in the Union, and, going abroad, degrades our character as a nation, as it most certainly and most vilely caricatures it, even its vulgarest part, — or were he, as a dramatist, to make a Wilton carpet pass for wit, and pulling-off of doorplates and knockers a mark of humor, were his male characters in fact all rogues or profligates, and his female, amazons or flirts and fools, he would be one of the fraternity of American popular authors, and perhaps might be stereotyped in England; but he writes English, and the men he holds up to imitation are men of honor as well as wit, and his women virtuous as well as vivacious, and for thus making us a race of civilized and honest and educated beings, as we are, instead of boors and blackguards, as we are not, and for attempting to improve the morals and amend the heart, instead of holding the mirror up to only the meanest part of nature, he deserves to be excommunicated; therefore he has been and is excommunicated; and the consequent and attendant step is damnation.

Staun. Well done, sir: you at least are not of his enemies, nor of the foes of wit.

Proof. [*sarcastically.*] Oh sir, what interest should I have; I am his publisher. Yet perhaps, you may praise me too, for [*lowering his voice.*], if the report is true, that his own father hates him for differing from common men, I certainly deserve some credit.

Staun. What is that you say? his own father? But that reminds me, that I have much to ask you about him, and others in this city. In the first place tell me, however, what made you show so much surprise, when this young gentleman ordered his books to be sent over the way?

Proof. His books, sir? Why, did you hear the names! They are all on painting, and the arts connected, and mostly rare and recondite books too. Why the deuse should they be sent to that house, where — hum! [*stopping short.*

Staun. Because, perhaps, he has found it a better situation for his paint-room — for his study.

Proof. For his study! [*chuckling.*] — booh! Do you know what my gentleman goes there for, sir? [*Lowering his voice.*] He keeps a —

Staun. Model. It is essential to an artist.

Proof. O, very! But he does not want to teach her painting, — or, at any rate, to teach her its abstruser principles out of Italian, French, and German authors. But that is not all, sir. You noticed his gloomy abstraction, as he went up the street. Then he seemed disconcerted at the amount of his purchase. I am afraid something is going wrong with —— [*checking himself, cautiously.*] You are a stranger; pardon me.

Staun. Going wrong with the family, you meant to say. O never mind me; I am no gossip. But I think you are over-fanciful. This, depend upon it, is some whim of the son's. It is nothing strange that an independent young man should prefer to have his rooms separate from his father's household. But what is this girl you speak of? I thought I heard her sing; and there was something in the song that woke response from an old note in my heart long out of tune; and I had meant to ask you about your neighbor, No. 92. But I trespass on your time. [*seeing Proof. waiting an opportunity to rise.*

Proof. No sir, no sir. I was only about to tell the boy, who was signaling to me that he was ready, to wait a moment. With your permission. [*rising.*

Staun. Certainly: but there is no need of detaining him. Have the goodness to have put up all the volumes we were speaking of. I will go into the shop and pay you for them; and while they are getting ready, we can finish our conversation.

Proof. Much obliged to you, sir. The boy shall take your parcel likewise, first leaving that for Miss Stockton, that you may see the house as you desire. [*They leave their seats together.*

Staun. One moment. [*stopping Proof.*] Have you no more knowledge of this girl?

Proof. O none whatever. In fact I have never seen her:

I but repeat a rumor I heard for the first time from old Stockton's bookkeeper; and certainly young Mr. Stockton is over the way constantly.

Staun. That will do. My other inquiries can be made as well in the shop. [*They pass into the shop; and the scene closes.*

SCENE III.

The parlor — as in Act I. Sc. I.

CLARA *is seen, with her*
eyes fixed upon the door, as if expecting somebody.
Enter LEDGER.
He bows respectfully, and with timidity (Clara returning his
courtesy with eyes cast down) and approaches in
the same manner, yet with a look of
marked tenderness.

Ledg. [*with embarrassment.*] Miss Stockton — I understood — desired to see me — before I should wait upon Mr. Stockton.

Clara. O Mr. Ledger! there is some dreadful mischief plotting against my father's peace and — and the peace of others connected with him. A letter it seems, from some unknown quarter, has disclosed to him my brother's hasty marriage, and, at the same time, has — has —— [*Throwing off all em-barrassment by a sudden effort.*] Why should I not be can-did? — and the time presses. Mr. Ledger, it couples — your name and my own [*Ledg. betrays an emotion of pleasure: Clara looks confused and turns aside her head.*] in some way — I know not what: but in short, my father is in great dis-pleasure; and it was in the heat of this passion that he sent for you. Be on your guard, then. Be —— Go now; do not stay to thank me.

Ledg. One moment, Miss Stockton. That any accident should couple my humble name ——

Clara. O this unmeaning gallantry! which, too, I ought not to permit from you, and which you have never yet —— But go; my father expects you.

Ledg. One word. — Fear not [*as she is going.*] — I will not presume even to thank you for this kind caution. — There is, Miss Stockton, a viler plot still than any that can concern your brother or even — or even me. I have come, deter-mined to reveal it to Mr. Stockton in time to save him from great loss; but as he perhaps will refuse to listen to me, now especially, and to the prejudice of Mr. Schurk ——

Clara. Schurk? He is! —— Go on, go on; for Heaven's sake! I hear my mother's step. [*In her anxiety, she presses close up to Ledger.*

Ledg. I have discovered that false entries ——

Enter MRS. STOCKTON.
She looks surprised, and grieved, — but not angry.

Mrs. S. [*gravely, but not unkindly.*] Mr. Ledger, you

forget that Mr. Stockton wants you immediately. Come, Clara.

Ledg. O madam, do you hear me: a serious discovery — Mr. Schurk —

Mrs. S. [*with displeasure.*] Mr. Ledger !

Clara. O hear him, mother !

Mrs. S. No, Mr. Stockton will hear him. Come, my daughter.

> [*Exeunt Clara and Mrs. S. at one side, while Ledger watches them with an air of affliction. As they are about to disappear from the scene, Clara turns her head round, for the first time, and for a single instant, as if by an uncontrollable impulse, and meets the eyes of Ledger. He manifests a silent transport.*

Ledg. [*going, at the opposite side.*] The first time —— O never to be forgotten ecstasy ! Now, come what will from her father, God be thanked ! [*Exit.*

[29] Scene IV.

The room, as in Act I. Sc. II.— Stockton *discovered
sitting before the fire, with his back to the table, his feet on the
pan of the grate, his arms folded, and his head
bent down on his breast ; his whole attitude indicating
a gloomy abstraction.*

Enter,
Ledger *preceded by* Hans.

Hans. Mr. Ledger, sir. [*Exit. He closes the door firmly to,
yet Stockton does not move. Ledger stands, hat in hand, half-
way between the door and the table. After waiting some moments :*

Ledg. [*respectfully, yet firmly ; at the same time, placing the
large keys of the countinghouse on the table.*] Mr. Stockton ; I
have brought the keys with me, and await your commands.
[*Stock. turns round, and looks at Ledg. for a moment steadily.
Ledg. returns the look with like steadiness, yet deferentially.*

Stock. Oh ! Mr. Ledger. — Sit down, sir. Draw your
chair to the table. [*Stock. drawing his own to the table in like
manner, so that they now are seated facing one another.*] Mr.
Ledger [*in a mild, but very grave tone, and very slowly.*] — You
have been now five years, I think, in my employ.

Ledg. Yes, sir.

Stock. [*in same tone, and with like steadiness, his eyes all the*
8*

while fixed steadily on Ledger's, and his hands clasped together, his arms being stretched at length on the table, toward Ledg.]
In all that time, have you ever had to complain of me, in any one respect as regards my duty as your principal? No protestations! Answer me simply, Yes or No.

Ledg. No, sir.

Stock. [*still same manner.*] Have I not been more to you than a conscientious and kind principal? Have I not, for the last two years, encouraged your intimacy with my only son, and made you welcome at all times, and on all occasions, in my family, as a favored visitor and friend?

Ledg. [*greatly moved.*] O Mr. Stockton! for God's sake ——

Stock. [*same mild and sad tone.*] Answer me simply, Henry: is this true, or is it not?

Ledg. It is true.

Stock. [*still same manner.*] You are a man honorable and good; you have too much sense not to understand that this unusual favor, this free admittance to my household, implied certain tacit conditions, and too much virtue not to have observed them as faithfully as if they had been written out and subscribed to. [*Ledg. bends his head over upon his hand, his elbow on the table.*] Be so good as to read that letter. [*in a rather higher tone, but still without severity.*

Ledg. [*indignantly, after perusing it.*] It is the handwriting of Schurk!

Stock. Sir, sir! — But there is no love lost between you. He said that you would say so, and found, himself, a strange resemblance in some of the characters.

Ledg. O no, Mr. Stockton; it is not that, for the hand

is disguised: it is the style, the general manner of the writing.

Stock. Enough. You have read it, I presume: [*With the sarcastic tone of smothered indignation.*] will you do me the honor to say, if the news it imparts is correct?

Ledg. [*with embarrassment.*] Mr. Stockton, it is impossible for me to say what may be the malice of society, or to answer the mean insinuations of a cowardly ——

Stock. [*giving way to his indignation.*] Don't talk of meanness, sir; what is this evasion of your own? this contemp ——

Ledg. [*hastily, yet with much dignity.*] There is no evasion. I am as open, Mr. Stockton, as yourself, or even, I am proud to say it, as your son.

Stock. Don't name him, sir; you are paired together in this — this accursed letter! [*crushing it violently together, and throwing it fiercely to the floor. Rising quickly, and speaking with a fierce determination, that is moreover evident in his compressed lips, his dilated nostrils and flashing eyes.*] You are open, you say. Very good: will you answer me a plain question? Do you —— [*With an effort.*] Have you, sir, an affection for my daughter?

Ledg. [*who has also risen.*] Mr. Stockton, I will convince you of my openness. I might evade your question by the expression of an ordinary gallantry; but I answer you — *I have.*

Stock. [*in a fury.*] O you have, sir? And have you ever acknowledged it to her?

Ledg. Never.

Stock. [*eagerly; with surprise, and with manifestly abated passion.*] On your honor, young man ?

Ledg. On my honor, — nor have ever dreamed to. Why needs that, Mr. Stockton ? I am known no liar.

Stock. I know it; but I am a father. [*His passion is entirely gone; but he speaks with much agitation.*] And there has — you must pardon me, Henry, it is my daughter, my only daughter, mind you — there has nothing ever passed between you that excited hopes in your breast ?

Ledg. [*casting down his eyes and hesitating.*] You should not have asked me what to answer must either make me appear a coxcomb, or make of me an actual betrayer of more than my own secrets.

Stock. It is then true ! O my God, my God ! [*beating his forehead. He walks to and fro in the front of the scene for a minute or two; then, turning back to Ledg.*] Once more ; and with the same frankness. Has this been often ? I mean, that your presumptuous hopes have been flattered.

Ledg. [*offended.*] Presumption, sir, is not what any man can accuse me of, with justice. [*Stock. stamps impatiently.*] However, to relieve your feelings as a father, Mr. Stockton, I assure you on my honor that I never have had hopes at all. Were indeed Miss Stockton not too noble to forget her duties, Henry Ledger has not forgotten his place, or the debt of gratitude he owes her father.

Stock. [*grasping his hand.*] Now God reward you ! you are a noble fellow, Henry.

Ledg. [*coldly, and withdrawing his hand.*] Stop, Mr. Stockton; one word more, and then you know *all ;* understand me,

ALL. What was in my mind, when just now I hesitated to answer you, is this : — I, sir — [*greatly embarrassed.*] — It is very hard ! — but I must speak, to prevent all misconstruction when you come hereafter to recall this scene. —

Stock. Right; go on, go on.

Ledg. I have never had hopes; there has nothing ever passed between Miss Stockton and — her father's clerk [*with slight asperity.*], that that father might not have witnessed, or the world at large could have put the least construction on as more than mere friendship. But once, and once only, and very recently, for one brief instant, — a single instant sir, and we parted, — did I fancy — a show of interest in Miss Stockton's manner towards me.

Stock. Enough. Sit down, Mr. Ledger. [*They both resume their seats at the table, and Stockton looks earnestly in Ledger's face, who meets his look with calmness and a modest dignity.*] Mr. Ledger — Let me call you Henry, and my friend — You must be aware, Henry, that it will be proper for all parties that your intimacy in my family should cease [*Ledg. drawing himself up with a slight emotion of pride.*] — do not be offended; it is for your good, as for — that of others. Mr. Schurk and you do not well agree; and after what has just now passed between us, it will be long before I can feel otherwise than unpleasant, perhaps embarrassed at your presence in the countingroom. Messieurs Cabot & Herbert, kind and very liberal men, are in want of a bookkeeper; and if you say so, I will make arrangements with them to-morrow for you, with a considerable increase of salary. I was prepared to take this step before your manly acknowledgments — which,

young man, I never shall forget, or cease to honor you for —
and therefore made out this check for $3000. As it is not of
your own motion, but mine, that you leave me before the
completion of the year, it is simple justice, Henry, that I pay
you for the entire term. [*extending the check.*

Ledg. [*drawing back, proudly, yet respectfully.*] The offer of
your interest with Messieurs Cabot & Herbert I am not too
proud to accept, Mr. Stockton; and I do it gratefully. As for
the check, the sixth part of the amount I believe I am entitled
to, and will therefore take as my right; but I can accept
nothing as a gratuity. — If however you would make a
return for my open dealing, I pray you, Mr. Stockton, to hear
what I have to disclose of Mr. Schurk.

Stock. No, no, not a word. — It is time indeed, that one
of you left me! this mysterious quarrel ——

Ledg. Excuse me for interrupting you, but there is no quarrel, and no ill-feeling, at least on my part: but I have discovered, in the actual discharge of my duties, that this very bad
man ——

Stock. [*angrily.*] Silence, sir, and if you have nothing more
to say than to abuse that excellent and pious gentleman, I
must wish you good evening. [*bowing.*

Ledg. [*retiring.*] Good evening, and farewell, Mr. Stockton.
You will repent of this. [*Coming quickly back.*] Yet once
more — I cannot see you in this danger without urging you,
if you will not listen to me, to ask ——

Stock. [*who has appeared much irritated all the while.*] O sir,
I am not used to take counsel of my clerks. Good night.
[*turning his back on Ledg.*

Ledg. Ah, this is! —— Well sir, you will yet learn. Good night. [*Exit.*

Stock. Why my whole family is mad, including myself and my two head-clerks. But yet [*musing.*], this young man is too conscientious and honorable to make a false accusation and too high-spirited to bear malice. There may be something. — I must read that letter again. [*Going hastily to lift it; and,*

while he is making this movement,

the Drop falls.

Act the Third

³⁰ Scene I. *In the house " No. 92 ". — A plainly,
yet not meanly, furnished parlor. A slender easel, with a small
canvas on it is seen at one side, as if put out
of the way. A guitar case.
An old fashioned pianoforte, &c. &c.*

Theresa,
*seated at a writing-table, on which is seen a
small inlaid desk, is rolling up what appears to be a Ms.*

Enter Clara,
cloaked, &c., as coming from the street.

Clara. [*running up and kissing Ther. fondly.*] What, always
scribble, scribble, scribble! Well, that is better than stitch,
stitch, stitch, — though, by and by, when you get a little
household, my girl, you 'll have enough of that too. But
what is that you have there? have not taken to book-making,
Therry? Have a care! you must not trespass on the preroga-
tive of your lord and master, my poet and painter brother.

Ther. [*putting the roll into a drawer of the table.*] Not for
the world. But don't ask me any questions, now, Clara dear;
you shall know all in time; and do not say anything to
Arthur about this.

Clara. No? secrets already? Well I won't; for one thing

I am sure of, whatever you are about is not, and never can be, anything naughty. There! am I not a good soul, and a most caressing sister?

Ther. Good you always have been [*kissing her.*], and caressing you must be, Clara, more than ever, both to Arthur and to me, to make him forget the evil I have brought upon him without my will, and me that I shall see it. But let me take off your things. [*offering to untie Clara's bonnet.*

Clar. No, I have but a minute to stay; *Peter waits me below. I have come expressly to keep up my brother's spirits; all I know will be right again very soon: papa is too good, and this gust of passion too sudden and too violent not to soon blow over; and then, Therry dear, we shall have you, and Arthur —— [*suddenly confused and blushing.*] There is somebody coming up the stairs.

Ther. Arthur: — but no, it is not his step.

Clar. O no, it is ——

Enter LEDGER.
He looks at first delighted, but directly recovers himself, and bows distantly to Clara, who, on her part, at first equally moved with himself, seems surprised at this change of mood and returns his courtesy slightly and stiffly.

Ledg. I was in hopes, Mrs. Stockton, to have found your husband with you. Do you know where he is? I must see him within the hour on a matter of the utmost importance.

Ther. I don't know where he is, Mr. Ledger; but he can-

not be out long. If you will but sit down —— Ah, that
is he, now! [*moving delightedly to the door. Ledg. hurries to
open it; and*

Enter ARTHUR.

Arth. My dear Ledger! Ah, sister! [*taking their hands in
turn.*] Theresa. — This looks pleasant for the evening of so
stormy a day to me.

Ledg. A storm, however, that has blown its worst, and
that is about to be succeeded, I am almost sure, by a season
of perfect happiness. Stockton, I am certain I know the
author of that letter: it is ——

Clara. [*eagerly.*] Mr. Schurk.

Ledg. Beyond a doubt, Miss Stockton. It has effected his
purpose against me, as against your brother; but it will not
avail him now.

Arth. What is this? How are you involved?

Ledg. Your father has but this moment dismissed me from
his employ.

Clara. Ah, I did not know you had such good cause to
be — unfriendly. [*She has moved near to him on the impulse
communicated by his last words, while Arth. simultaneously has
grasped his hand.*

Ledg. Cause? and unfriendly? It is now only that you do
me wrong, Miss Stockton. If, on seeing you, I checked myself, and bowed with restraint, it is, because Mr. Stockton —
because your father — [*embarrassed.*

Arth. [*while Clara looks confused, and seems fearful of
Ledger's reply.*] Has what?

Ledg. In very plain words, he has forbid me his house. [*Arth. in the extremity of his surprise seems incapable of speech, and Clara's embarrassment increases. Ledg. continues hastily, as if afraid to be interrupted.*] Under these circumstances, of course, the friendly address I had hitherto been permitted to adopt towards Miss Stockton —

Arth. Was not in the least to be modified — not here, if in my father's house. As my sister, Clara must still welcome the friend of her brother; as my father's daughter, she will perform her duties as her own conscience and her knowledge of those duties may dictate. But proceed, dear Ledger; let us to the bottom of this mystery at once. Schurk is a villain; that is taken for granted by every one here: well?

Ledg. And will be acknowledged by your father before midnight. — But Miss Stockton must forgive me [*to Clara.*]: I was about, but a minute or two ago, to reveal to her what now, for the very same reason, her father's interest, I must conceal. Mr. Stockton, after the hints I have vainly thrown out to him to-night, can not remain easy, he will seek for information from Mrs. Stockton and yourself: to know any-thing more than you now know would defeat our plans, and you must have ignorance, dear Miss Stockton, to be able to plead it.

Arth. Yes, go, Clara; Ledger is right, we may be sure, whatever his reason.

Clara. [*gayly.*] [32] O never fear, brother; I have no pride to be shocked: you gentlemen may be as close as you please. Come Therry, let us leave the owls to their own tu-whooing; we have secrets of our own, my girl, quite as interesting, —

at least, one of us has. [*looking significantly at Ther. and then at the drawer, — Ther. returning the look by one of entreaty, — Arth. not observing.*] Come, now, light me carefully down these dark stairs of yours : it is to be for the last time I hope. [*as they move off.*] You see I was sure all would go well. *Au revoir*, brother. Good night, [*more gravely, and diffidently.*] Mr. Ledger. [*Exeunt Clar. and Ther., the gentlemen bowing them to the door in silence, — Ledg. with his eyes bent down, as if afraid to trust himself.*

Arth. And now, Ledger ? [*taking both his hands in his.*

[33] *Ledg.* Through circumstances there is no time now to relate, I became possessed of one fact which obliged me to examine privately Mr. Schurk's accounts, when I discovered that for some time past he has, by means of false entries, abstracted large sums from your father, amounting now to no less than $138,000.

Arth. Ah ! And so trusted by my father ! Go on.

Ledg.[34] My manner, since this discovery, must have been sufficiently suspicious to a guilty man like Schurk, not to say that every new hour he was more and more in danger of detection by his master. Of course, to get rid of me was essential for immediate safety ; but that would avail him little unless you were also removed. Hence the letter, which I recognized immediately for his German hand, and perhaps Mr. Stockton might have also, had he not been partially blinded by his passionate resentment of your marriage, Arthur, and been put off the scent by Schurk himself, who it seems had pointed out the resemblance himself to your father, and warned him that I would perceive it.

Arth. Well done, Heiliger !

Ledg. Yes, hypocrite as well as knave. Well, to-day there arrived $11,000 in specie from China, consigned to your father in behalf of a Mr. Staunton, who came on, I understand, in the same ship with it to New York. Schurk has resolved desperately to carry it off, and this very night.

Arth. [*in extreme surprise.*] Impossible !

Ledg. It does indeed seem a gratuitous hardihood. There may be some other villany meditated besides the robbery; and there may be causes —— However, he has actually tampered with honest Guterknecht, who, by my advice, half promised to assist him, by procuring the keys of the counting-house. But I hear the good old German's steps, now. As I passed him in the hall, I gave him a hint to meet us both here.

Enter HANS.

Arth. Well, my good Hans. So you are preparing for the state-prison ?

Hans. Ah, my dear Mr. Artur; dis ist no matter for jesting.

Ledg. Not to your countryman, Hans; but to us it is: we had never cause to be more pleasant. Your master will be rid of a great rogue, Mr. Arthur will be restored to favor ——

Arth. Do not be too sure of that; there is more than the letter between my father and me. However,[35] let us see what is now to be done. You are to get the keys for Schurk, I understand. [*to Hans.*] They of course let others in, besides the robbers. Thence defeat to their plans, and Schurk revealed in his true character. What more ?

Hans. I 'm to meet Mr. Schurk dis fery minute in a little out of the way tavern, where nobody but Germans, and fery poor Germans, goes. If you could go dere too, I could make him talk English — you might hear more dan you tink for.

Arth. Excellent! Ledger? But you shake the head.[36] I see, my dear fellow, you would object to this eavesdropping; and who can detest it more than I? but remember the emergency.

Ledg. Yes, but there is more than my natural reluctance. Consider, Stockton, you want a better witness of Schurk's villany than one like myself who have lost place through him. You yourself are partly unfitted for the business; I should be still worse. I am ready for the surprise of the robbers; but you had better — must indeed, get some impartial person to take my place in this affair.

Arth. Very true. Let me see. Oh, there is Buzz, the great author that is making such a stir among us. He, you know, dived into the Coalholes of the Five Points in New York, and found himself quite in his element: he 'll be perfectly enraptured to make one on this occasion.

Ledg.[37] It will serve him too to enliven his " American Notes ", which he is to get out in imitation of the still more famous *Bozz*. But where to find him on the instant?

Arth. He was to accompany my publisher to hear my tragedy hissed to-night. He will probably be at his shop now. Let us off. Hans, you shall tell us on the way where we are to find this tavern of yours, and all else we need to know and be prepared for. Come, Ledger; my father, *prodigal* as he thinks me in my own affairs, shall find that I am not negligent or slothful in his.   [*Exeunt.*

Scene II.

Same as in Act II. Sc. II.

Staunton, Buzz, *and* Proofsheet.

Buzz. What! will you deny me the use of my own eyes? [*to Staun.*

Staun. No; but I say you use them badly, and your pen still worse.

Buzz. How, the devil! did n't I see the pig myself, and the little fellow on top of him, both as large as life, and in the very heart of Broadway?

Staun. Possibly; but how have you set it down?

Proof. [*to Staun., while Buzz is lugging out an enormous memorandum-book, and hunting up the passage.*] Just as any other traveling Englishman would do.

Staun. [*to Proof.*] I forgive you that hit, for the sake of its present applicability.

Buzz. You shall see. Here it is: I 'll be judged by the Americans themselves [*looking to the audience.*] of the truth of the picture. "In New York, the little boys, of all classes, are

taught pork-riding, as their sisters are pork-feeding.   Is a little
shaver sent by his mamma to buy a stick of molasses-candy, —
called there, by the old-fashioned, *cockeenia*, and affectionately,
cockyninny, — for the baby or for company, his sister holds a
turnip-top, or the like, over the kennel before the house-door:
up come a herd of grunters at once ; the rider gives a twist in
the tail of the one that suits him, swings himself on its back,
then lays fast hold by the ears, and off they go, the boy's legs
banging his bristly charger all the way, till the end of the
journey, when the express is dismissed and another taken for
the return.   There can be no question, I think, that in the
event of another war these youthful riders, brought up thus
early to porcination, will become formidable cavalry-officers."

Staun. And you put that down for fact ?

Buzz. No, for conclusions.   I don't make my fact : the pig
was there —

Staun. With his tail all curled.

Buzz. Sir! With the boy on top of him.   And I make my
conclusions that porcination takes the place, in republican
America, of equitation.

Staun. As more natural, and saving a great expense in
saddlery.

Buzz. All philosophers, sir, draw conclusions.   There is
Lyell, the great geologist: he puts it down in his book that
the pigs in the streets of Cincinnati are public property ; and,
when anybody wants a roaster, he sallies out, knife in
hand ——

Staun. And his wife with a bucket of hot water ; and the
throat is cut, and the hide is scalded —

Proof. In the presence of the Mayor and Common Council.

Enter

ARTHUR, *followed by* HANS.

Mr. Stockton, you 're just in time for the tail. Will you have it soused?

Arth. Souse? and *tails?* and Pickins seems quite in a pickle! — But I cannot wait an explanation. Buzz, if you will off with me, I 'll show you a scene that will fit your drama of the Five Points.

Buzz. What, another *break-down?* [*Dances, heel and toe, a double-shuffle, and sings, " O jump, Jim Crow, O jump, Jim Crow!" or whistles the tune, as an accompaniment.*] But I 'm one with Proof. here, for your new tragedy.

Arth. Never mind that; it will keep, if it live at all, for another night; and if not, there is no need of you at the execution. I want you, to help ensnare one of the greatest rascals in Philadelphia.

Buzz. Ah! a personification of Repudiation.

Arth. [*coolly.*] No, nor of the opponents of copyright either. Yet it might well be of both; for it is one of the Old Country I mean, that has settled among us for the benefit of the lawyers. We are about to track him to a sort of den.

Buzz. A lion, eh! I must get my pistols.

Proof. Allow me to suggest, your " American Notes " will answer — if the beast has brains.

Arth. We don't want either, but only your ears. It is a fox, or a wolf at worst, no lion, not at least this hunt.

VOL. V.—9

Buzz. Well, I 'm with you. It may give me a fresh villain for my portfolio. [*Exeunt Arth. and Buzz, followed by Hans. Buzz heard singing, as he passes through the shop,* "O jump, Jim Crow, O &c."

Proof. For the world are pretty well sick of the old, re-vamped Ralph-Ticklemies, and Chucklewits.

Staun. Or should be.— And it is such fellows as this, Mr. Proofsheet, that keep my country and yours perpetually in hot water!

Proof. Why not, sir? They say your bulldog must be fed with offal, to keep him in a fighting humor.

Staun. Or a growling one. That 's because his feeders have accustomed him to nothing wholesome.[38] However, Mr. Stockton seems to have very little of the anxiety about his piece that authors usually display.

Proof. O he is above all that, sir; and if his piece were damned to-night, I am sure he would not even shrug his shoulders, but merely set to work to write another. Yet he is a man of very ardent feelings too. But in the present case, you may depend upon it, there is something very serious.

Staun. True, he seemed very earnest and grave when he lugged off the admirer of *Jim-Crow.* And the old Dutchman behind him —

Proof. Who is his father's body-servant, a man of great trust, and besides not given to trifling —

Staun. Yes, this old fellow's brows were as gloomy and his whole face as sad as a mute's at a funeral. But —— Ah! here is a brighter vision.

Enter

from the shop, timidly and hesitatingly, preceded by a shopboy,
THERESA.

The boy points to PROOFSHEET, *bows, and retires.*

STAUNTON *takes up his hat, keeping his eyes the whole time
fixed upon Theresa, and appears to be about moving, but
hesitates, and remains, simply drawing back a little.*

Ther. [*with distressing diffidence, scarcely able to speak.*]   A
little manuscript, sir, [*offering a roll to Proof.*] which, if it suit
you, I should be glad to — to dispose of.

Proof. [*taking it carelessly.*]   Sorry ma'am — but really —
we are so overrun with engagements of this nature.   A story
is it? [*beginning to unroll it.*

Ther. Yes, a simple narrative — for children.

Proof. Hum! am afraid — been so much lately of the sort
in the market —— We might publish it indeed for you, if you
thought it worth while.

Ther. [*anxiously.*] Do you mean ——

Proof. In the usual manner.   You print it; we sell it for
you on the customary terms of thirty-three and a third per
cent. [*Ther. extends her hand faintly for the roll, appearing
much distressed.   Staun. brushes forward, and, with the
greatest deference bowing to Ther., intercepts it.*

Staun. If you will permit me, young lady: I might perhaps —— [*beginning to unroll it.*

Ther. Are you a publisher, sir?

Staun. No, not exactly a publisher; but I ——

Proof. O, he is a Mæcenas — a patron of letters. You could not do better, madam —

Staun. [*looking severely at Proof.*] Perhaps not — than entrust it to my hands. But will you not be seated? [*extending, with marked respect, a chair to Ther., who declines it timidly.*] No? Well, I will detain you but a minute. [*reading the title.*] " The Schoolmistress and her Pupils." Ah! I think I should like this [*pretending to look over some of the leaves.*] — am very sure I should. Will you leave it with me for an hour or two? I am almost certain I can find you a liberal purchaser for the manuscript, if I do not undertake its publication myself.

Ther. O sir, how shall I? —— [*but she looks at Proof., who is eying Staun. with an expression of droll surprise, as if he suspected him of a joke, and her voice falls.*] but I fear, sir, — that —

Staun. [*looking up, and catching the glance of Ther. and the expression of Proof.*] That I am bantering you. Young lady, I have not been long enough in the trade for that. [*with a severe glance at Proof., who shrugs his shoulders, and composes his countenance directly.*] If you will leave me your address, you shall be convinced of that by to-morrow.

Ther. [*embarrassed.*] I — I thank you, sir — but — I would prefer to send for your decision, if you will say when.

Staun. As early then to-morrow, as may suit yourself. Allow me. [*handing her politely through the door of the room leading into the shop. Proof. puts himself forward, as if ashamed to be outdone.*] No sir, this is now my office. [*Exeunt, through the shop, Staun. and Ther.*

Proof. [*after following them with his eyes a few moments.*]

My gentleman is either a very great fool, or a very great rogue. These Englishmen are certainly odd fish. — But it is time to be off. [*looking at his watch.*] Francis [*calling into the shop.*], is Mr. Copy gone? Yes? You may begin to fasten up then.

Re-enter STAUNTON.

Staun. How could you be so cruel to that young creature?

Proof. Cruel? I acted but in my trade, Mr. Staunton.

Staun. Trade? And does that forbid you bowels?

Proof. Very generally, for any other books than our own, which are — our daybooks. But what is *your* compassion, sir? Will this young woman be any better for it to-morrow?

Staun. I think she will. — What is usually given for a manuscript of this character, supposing it of course to be respectable as a composition?

Proof. [*looking over it.*] Forty pages — a juvenile. Twenty-five dollars. If something *very* extraordinary, it might be fifty.

Staun. I shall give her one hundred and fifty; and if I find it readable, you shall publish it besides at my expense; so that her need, as I think it, and her pride will both be satisfied.

Proof. I think not. If she has pride, you will revolt it directly, by such an enormous offer, — perhaps make her suspect you besides. [*looking at him scrutinizingly.*

Staun. [*Indignant.*] Good God, sir! — But have a care! If you knew what feeling that timid girl has excited in me by a fancied resemblance — you would not dare —— [*checking himself.*] I am wrong.

Proof. Whether wrong or not, Mr. Staunton, it is none of my business. But if you are serious, you would do well not to give this sum, but to act as a publisher would under like circumstances. Tell this lady, that you would gladly give her $100, but that there is really so much competition, and the risk is so considerable, and the remuneration so trifling —

Staun. In short, any other of the — cant of the trade —

Proof. The *lies*, I think you meant to say. [*bowing.*] But we will not quarrel — I really am ready to serve you in this matter, which you seem to have at heart. — That you can only afford, at present, $75. You can then print it, if you will; the expense will be in all about $50; and giving her the remaining twenty-five, as her share of the profits, you have your one hundred and fifty disposed of, without leading the authoress to suspect that she is dealing with any but a man of business.

Staun. You are very right. I will do so. You shall write in my name just such a note as you think proper and have it ready for the lady when she sends for it to-morrow.

Proof. [*who has had his eye musingly fixed upon the Ms., which lies upon the table.*] And have you any idea, sir, who is this lady ?

Staun. Idea? Surely not! [*Eagerly.*] Have you?

Proof. I have very little doubt, it is the very person we were speaking of. You see, by this title, that the work purports to be a record of the proper experience of a young schoolmistress with her pupils. Well, it is only six weeks since the little sign of " Dayschool for Young Ladies " was taken down from 92, opposite; and there has been, I am pretty sure, no change of tenants there.

Staun. And this was the reason why, when she left me at the shopdoor, she made, at first, a step or two, as if to cross the street, then came back, and hesitatingly turned down the street, as if she wanted to conceal from me where she was going. I took it indeed for a hint to that effect, and came in. Well, if this is so, you must acknowledge that this young girl — besides that it would be sin to suspect her of impurity — can not be the mistress of young Stockton, or what could she need to sell her labor for ?

Proof. True, and ladies of that class are not apt to be literary. But you seem to be particularly interested, Mr. Staunton ? [*inquisitively.*

Staun. I am; I might pretend, because I am about to make a literary *protegée* of her: but I confess to you, there is something in this young girl's look, and mien, which, with a peculiar incident of a well-known song that I have little doubt I heard her sing this very evening — a song I have but too good cause to remember, seems to connect her, in spite of myself, with the secret object of my visit to this country. [*Proof. looks astonished.*] It is a matter altogether of a private nature ;[39] but I tell you thus much, — which will convince you, that if you can ascertain to-morrow anything about her you will oblige me, — that it was in the endeavor to discover the fair singer of No. 92, that I did not go with your boy to Mr. Stockton's just now. I happened to see, at the time, a lady, followed by a servant, go into the house opposite. She left her attendant at the door; and I waited, only to be disappointed; for after a while she came out again : so that it was but a visitor.   Besides, my man ascertained from her servant, that the lady was no other than Miss Stockton.

Proof. [*astonished.*] Indeed !   Then there is hardly a mistress in the case.   I do not understand this.

Staun. [*changing his manner to a cold gravity.*] I don't see why you need.   It is all simple.   Mr. Stockton visits there as a friend, and his sister likewise. — Still you may put some inquiries, if you like, to-morrow.   I must now make my visit to Mr. Stockton's father.

Proof. Visit ?   You know him then.

Staun. I think I do, though I have no knowledge of his family.   Will you let one of your boys call a carriage and direct it to the house ?

Proof. Readily.   But you had better walk, sir; the distance is very trifling: he shall show you the way.   You would not like then to see the first performance of Mr. Arthur Stockton's play ?   Mr. Pickins' not going leaves me a seat to spare.[40]   We shall be just at the opening of the first act. It is now half past eight; and a little musical piece was to precede the tragedy ; for the author so stipulated, in order that the effect of the drama might not be annulled by the usual sequel of a farce.

Staun. Thank you ; but I shall be in better mood another night.   Is your boy ready ? [*Putting on his hat and going to the shop.*

Proof. Yes, he only waits for us to leave, to put out the lights.   Francis [*following Staun. through the door.*]: you will show this gentleman to Mr. Stockton's.   [*Scene closes.*

SCENE III.

A vulgar tavern, half refectory, half tippling-shop, whose German character is indicated to the spectators by a scrawl in charcoal over the fireplace, as if done by some bacchanal, of " 𝔅𝔦𝔢𝔯𝔥𝔞𝔲𝔰" in German letters over a rude sketch of a mug and two crossed tobaccopipes: elsewhere, " 𝔚𝔦𝔯𝔱𝔥𝔰𝔥𝔞𝔲𝔰", and other significant inscriptions. The foreground is divided into boxes, back to back of one another, and separated by a partition so that both sides are seen from the house at once.

At a table on the right hand of the spectators ARTHUR *and* PICKINS *are discovered sitting; a stone beer-bottle and pewter mugs before them; but they do not drink. In the contiguous box, on the other side, by a similar table,* SCHURK *and* HANS; *the former so placed that his back is against the partition, while* HANS *sits opposite, on the other side of the table.* SCHURK *is smoking furiously from a long pipe, while a man is just arranging before them beer and mugs.*

Sch. [noisily.] [41] *Bier? Nein! nein! Branntwein — Weinbranntwein! [Man leaves them.*

Hans. So sei es. But you must talk English, or I vont sit here a moment : you vill ruin us bot'. [*smoking.*

Sch. Tändelei! but have it your own way. How do you know but some damned Yankee may hear us? And that will be as bad as ten Germans, I think.

Hans. Pah! Here? Yankees here? Vy, none but de

9*

most ignorant even of our countryman: come in dis place. Frenchmen perhaps — but none dat shpreak English. And s'pose dey do ; de chance ist less.

Sch. *Schon gut! schon gut!* [*The man returns, sets a bottle on the table and two glasses, and a waterpitcher.*] *Dank!* [*man retires. — Sch. pours out a glass, and offers to fill another for Hans, who shakes his head, holding up his mug to intimate his preference of beer.*] No? Well, brandy for me. [*Drinking down his portion at a breath.*] I took a tremendous horn before I came here ; for this business makes me cold.

Hans. Vy do you engage in it, den? 't is n't too late to back out.

Sch. [*violently, and striking his hand on the table.*] No? And to-morrow morning have my accounts examined by old Stockton, and all found out! To-night, to-night hides or discovers all. Drink! beer or brandy, as you please ; but drink, I say, — or you 'll make me suspect you.

Hans. Me? but I nefer do trink ; and vat I come here for, if you sushpect me?

Sch. Because I cannot do without you. But forgive me ; you are my countryman, you will do what I want. Will you get the keys, Hans?

Hans. De keys, [*hesitating.*] y — es. But five-hundred *thaler* ist very little money — for such a risk.

Sch. Say then one thousand. Will that do?

Hans. One tousendt. *Ach, ja!* I vill — I vill do it ; but remember, one tousendt!

Sch. Yes, yes. [*drinking.*] I wish to God it was over.

Hans. Vhen you vant de keys?

Sch. Very soon — in one hour — half after nine or ten — say ten o'clock; the street is dark and deserted, and we are as safe then as at midnight.

Hans. Besides, if we 're seen, nobody vill sushpect us two; we 've but to make known who we are.

Sch. So much for a good name. [*laughing coarsely, with an affected ruffianism.*]

Hans. No, for a goodt place. But Mr. Schurk, dis is a boldt scheme. Vhy you not get de money elseway — write Mr. Shtockton's name for example?

Sch. Forge, eh! Very good! but that will not save my reputation. I had one other game yet, but I could make nothing of it, and I played my last hand an hour ago. Could I have gained a wife, I might have had a father to wink at the errors in my bookkeeping, but — *dass sie der Donner und das Wetter erschlage!* [42] Miss Clara preferred another man. [*Arth. unable to restrain himself, half-rises from the table, Buzz holding him down, and a slight noise is thus occasioned.*] What's that? [*makes a movement to rise.*] I will see who 's there.

Hans. [*retaining him by the sleeve.*] *Pah!* it ist nobody, or nobody but a couple of stupid Frenchmans I heardt jabbering vhen we came in. Sit down; do you see how de host is vatching us? ve shall be sushpected.

Sch. Well, but this is a life and death matter; for I mean — [*Suddenly and with great earnestness and very quickly.*] [43] *Aber wenn du dann —— but if you should betray me! — Sieh da!* [*opening his vest and pointing significantly to the stock of a pistol.*]

Hans. Go on! haave I come here to trifle! Hide dat, and

don't let your badt temper betray you agin into sphreaking
Deutsch, or I 'll give up, and leaf you to get de keys where
you can.

Sch. Well, don't be angry, my good Hans; I can't but be
fearful: this is a terrible affair. Hark! [*taking Hans by the lapel
of the coat, and drawing him close to him, so that their faces
almost touch.*] do you think me such a fool as for a paltry
$11,000 to risk all, when I could make fifty times as much, as
you say, by a dash of the pen? [*Loosing his hold, yet speaking
with the same smothered earnestness, almost between his teeth.*]
When I go to rob —— [*beating his brow suddenly, — then in a
tone of despair.*] O this cursed gaming! to what it has sunk
me! [*buries his face in his hands. Then
drinking fiercely, and bursting out into the noisy hunting-song
of Der Freischütz, as if to drown his thoughts, or to give
him spirits:*

> " Was gleicht wohl auf Erden dem Jäger-Vergnügen,
> Wem sprudelt der Becher des Lebens so reich?
> Beim " — [41]

Hans. Why what ails you?

Sch. Not wine — nor beer — nor brandy; it is vice —
dishonor — death!

    [*Singing with renewed burst of desperate gayety, and
    smashing his pipe on the table.*] "Joho, trallala!" &c.

          [*as in the well-known chorus.*

But how sad you look! one might think you pitied me;
but you are deep in, yourself. Perhaps you don't like my
song. Let 's try one more wicked, but less noisy:

[*Singing.*] " Kartenspiel und Würfellust,
Und ein Kind mit runder Brust,
Hilft zum frohem Leben ! " [45]

No, no, no — cards and dice, if not the girls, have been too much for me already. I 'll drink no more, [*brushing bottles and glasses off the table.*] or I shan't be fit for business.

Hans. But vhat is dat? You have n't saidt, and I must know vhat you vill do.

Sch. Fire [*in an audible whisper.*]: there, do you understand *that?* the ashes, if we do the job well, will tell no tales.

Buzz. [*from the other side of the partition.*] A precious ras— [*Arth. claps his hand on his mouth. Buzz struggles and draws out his memorandum-book to make a note.*

Sch. [*springing up, and attempting to run down the scene to get to the other side of the partition.*] *Strafe mich Gott !* [46] There is some one there. I heard voices.

Hans. [*holding him back.*] De Frenchmans I tell you. You 'll ruin all.

Sch. [*Turning round and grasping Hans by the collar.*] Frenchmen? Have you dared? — But I 'll see that quickly. *Herr Wirth !* [47] [*calling to the landlord The latter enters from within and goes up. Schurk talks earnestly with him in a low voice, appears at length to be satisfied, and landlord retires to the right.*

Hans. Dere! I toldt you so; two paltry Frenchmans. But we haad better shtay here no longer — or we may shtay too long. [*rising.*

Sch. Ganz recht ! But remember the keys; ten o'clock precisely — *mit dem Schlag.*

Hans. And de tousendt.   Not one tollar less.

Sch. Ganz gewiss.   Auf! auf!   Mit dem Schlug zehn Uhr.
"Joho, trallala, &c." [*They retire down the scene.*

For a moment, Schurk appears to struggle with Hans and en-
deavor to get round the partition.   Hans seems to remon-
strate earnestly, and at last drags him off to the right.
Exeunt. —   Arth. and Buzz come down.

Arth. Good God! what a spectacle! [*in a tone of sadness*
and compassion.

Buzz. [*joyously.*] Yes, the finest in the world.   I must have
it set down — wait a moment [*writing in his note-book.*]:
"Not wine — nor beer — nor brandy [*repeating energetically*
Schurk's words.]; it is vice — dishonor — death!"   Were n't
those the words?

Arth. Yes, but had you known this man, you would see
nothing but matter of grief in all this.   His drinking — singing — all was novel, — the effect of mere desperation.

Buzz. That is what makes the spectacle. [*Continuing to*
write.] "Fire!   Do you hear that? the ashes will cover up
our tale!"   Was that it?

Arth. No, there was nothing about covering up tales.
Your head seems to be always running upon such
things.

Buzz. And with good reason; they have made my head
what it is, the most conspicuous, with the Duke of Wellington's[48] and one or two others, in the nation.   But, I say,
Stockton, the old fellow, your Hans, did his part bravely too,
with his *tousendt.*   "One tousendt!   *Ach, ja!*   I vill — I vill
do it; but remember, one tousendt!"   I never played Captain
Bobadil better.[49]   Quite to the life!

Arth. Yes, and you had like to cost him his life too. Come now, the way must be clear by this time ; let us go.

Buzz. There — I 'm ready. [*returning his book to his pocket.*] Ah, if you could have seen my Bobadil ! " It is the most fortunate weapon, [*repeating after the character.*] that ever rid on a poor gentleman's thigh. Shall I tell you, sir ? You talk of Morglay, Excalibur, Durindina, or so ! Tut, I lend no credit to that is fabled of 'em ; I know the virtue of mine own, and therefore I dare the boldlier maintain it."

Arth. It is very well, no doubt ; but, Pickins, this is not the proper stage.

Buzz. Well, I 'm ready. That was a good villain too ! " Why, what ails you ? — Not wine — nor beer — nor brandy ; it is vice — dishonor — death ! " A genteel villain, ruined by cards and dicing ; the world shall hear of him yet. Yet I could wish you had seen my Bobadil. A capital villain ! " *Joho, trallala* " — [*singing as Schurk.*]

        Exit with Arth., arm in arm, to the right.

ACT THE FOURTH

SCENE I.   *Stockton's private room, as in Act I. Sc. II.*

STOCKTON *and* STAUNTON.
The former impatiently walking up and down.

Staun. Patience. Do sit down, Stockton. [*Stock. sits.*] —
Do you remember when you first saw me in India?

Stock. Very well: it is just twelve years ago.

Staun. Just so; and I seemed to you? —

Stock. The saddest man I ever looked upon. There was
nothing that could make you smile.

Staun. And do you know why? My heart was breaking.[50]
You look surprised. Listen: my story is a brief one, and
could never be told to you at a better time than now. [*Stock.
looks incredulous and impatient.*] I am serious. — My father
was the youngest son of a family of rank, and his destiny, in
the aristocratic order of things, was the army or the church;
but he had a mind of his own, a very republican one too, took
a wife from the city, very rich and very beautiful, and em-
barked with his father-in-law in commerce. The inheritor of my
father's liberal notions as well as of his fortune, I too married,
not to please the Stauntons, but myself; and my wife too was
beautiful — very beautiful, Stockton, and very accomplished,
though indifferently off in worldly effects. As I was an only

child, so one alone, a girl, was the fruit of my own marriage;
yet I believed myself the happiest of men. I was so. What
has made you unhappy this day, made me superlatively
wretched for years.

Stock. [*with awakened attention.*] Ah?

Staun. Yet in directly bringing about this evil, ourselves,
we were governed by opposite motives; for what to you is
A Vice was to me then, and is again, *A Virtue.*

Stock. Your daughter then? — [*eagerly.*

Staun. No; she was but five years old. It was my wife.
In few words, Stockton. I took pleasure in gathering about
me men of talent: poets, artists of all kinds, all found my
house a home,[51] at which the worthier among them were more
than welcome, — at which they were, as they deserve to be,
caressed; and I loved to see their society elicit the fine faculties and noble tastes with which nature and education had
both liberally endowed my wife. Among the rest, was one
especially honored. The intimacy between him and Catharine
became closer than that of brother and sister. At first I felt
no alarm, though I knew they corresponded. But it came at
last. Marston had no outward attraction superior to my own,
nay, he squinted and stooped, but his voice was beyond all
comparison the most perfect I have ever heard; the mellowest
tones of the softest flute, when best played, were no extrava-
gant parallel. With my new feelings, to find day after day,
when I came home, my wife listening as if intoxicated, while
Marston read aloud some poem, either his own or the composition of some greater man, became to me a perfect torment:
the voice of the man himself sounded in my ears as the hiss

of a cobra. Why need I go through all the phases of my passion? it is the old story; jealousy, hatred, then — the thirst to kill. One evening, I found on entering the room my wife seated at the piano, singing in her touching tones a simple air of Lodoiska then popular — "Ye streams that round my prison creep." Marston stood at her right hand, looking delight. I took my place directly behind her. The music went on; yet I fancied there was some embarrassment in both, as if I had surprised them unpleasantly. I was all but mad: I stretched out my right hand, and bringing the middle finger and thumb together, struck him sharply with the nail of the former, as if in sport, upon the lobe of the ear. Catharine, if she observed it, might have thought it jest; but Marston, turning round, encountered my burning eyes, and my insulting grin. [52] He was a man of quick perception, and understood me directly; but he was also a man of courage, and made no observation there. The next morning in Old Bond-street, a man passed me, then, turning short about, came toward me. It was Marston. Lifting suddenly his hand, he struck me heavily with the palm of it on my shoulder. Anybody passing might have thought it a boisterous or vulgar mark of good-fellowship: but I understood him, the more so that he pointed with the tip of his finger to his ear, and his eyes seemed, as mine *felt*, as if they blazed. "Where shall I hear from you?" I said; "and when?" "Be at the Athenæum," he answered, "in an hour, or an hour and a half at most, with any friend; Captain Hazard of the Engineers will call on you in my behalf." The next day, Marston lay at my feet in a pool of his own blood. [*Gasping.*

Stock. Good God! take breath, Staunton.

Staun. [*recovering.*] It is over now. — I started for the Continent. My wife had been ordered, by a letter through my second, to meet me at Dover with our child. She was not told the cause. She came. What ensued I need not describe; but the next morning I found my wife and child had fled in the night, in the same postchaise that had brought them. A packet of letters lay on the table in their chamber. The address was to Catharine, the handwriting Marston's. Without a wish to open one of them, I enveloped and sealed them and sent them on to London, to the care of the banker who managed her little property. They reached her. Marston, I heard, was expected hourly to die. I durst not return to England; and I had no desire to; — for even my child was lost to me, for ever.

Stock. Merciful Heaven! — How was that?

Staun. Catharine was high-spirited, and romantic; perhaps vindictive. When I endeavored to ascertain her movements, I found no trace of them. Her little funds had been taken from the hands of her banker, who could give me no information. I went to India, where I had a partner actually resident. My presence there enabled him to return to England, and I remained, to lead — what life, you, Stockton, who became there my chief intimate and friend, well know.

Stock. True, Staunton, and it was my sole grief at leaving India that I left you no happier. But did you never hear again of your wife and child?

Staun. Never any but the vaguest tidings till last year, when there reached me from America, forwarded by my

partner in London — what think you? The packet of letters
I had found at Dover. They were in two envelopes; the
outer sealed with a black seal, altogether strange to me, and
addressed in a strange hand, but the inner endorsed simply with my name in Catharine's own hand and sealed with
her usual device.

Stock. And there was nothing written by her?

Staun. Not one word. If she was dead, she had carried
her resentment with her to the grave. But the letters,
Marston's letters, Stockton ——

Stock. You read them, then?

Staun. I did; to mourn my own delicacy, that I had not done
so before. They established the innocence of the poor fellow
completely; for even the last one, written within two days of
the duel, was purely literary. Their friendship, in fact, was
imprudent, my encouragement unwise; but there was no guilt.

Stock. And did Marston die?

[53] *Staun.* Strangely enough, I could never ascertain; but I
think that had such been his fate, I must have learned it. For
myself, I had gathered one fact, that the packet was originally
from Philadelphia; and I am here in consequence, to find at
least my child.

Stock. And to-morrow we will, together, take the most
effectual measures for that purpose.

Staun. And to-morrow, Stockton, you will receive back
your child — your son? [*laying his hand on Stock.'s shoulder
imploringly.*

Stock. No, no! [*impatiently.*] Once more, do not urge me:
our cases have nothing in common.

Stock. Pardon me, they have much in common ; and I have seen your son, and heard that of him that makes me think, that, were he mine, I should be the proudest father on earth.

Stock. [*half-maliciously.*] Because you are a patron of letters as well as merchant. [*Staun. looks at him reproachfully.*] — Forgive me ; but you don't know how you gall me. Tell me, [*quickly.*] — were you to find your daughter, would you give her to such a man as my son, — her an heiress, as she then must be, to one who has nothing but his brains to call his own ?

Staun. Give her ! Ay, and my heart with her : [54] I should hold it the happiest day of my life. Nay, listen, Stockton ; though I never will seek to control the affections of my daughter, should I find her, and — God help me ! [*sighing.*] find her all that I *would* find her — yet, if she will be guided by my preferences, she never will marry any but a man of letters.

Stock. [*with slight sarcasm.*] Because this *Vice*, as I hold it in my only son, is to you, who have no son, a *Virtue*. Well then, I have not told you all : if I have cast off the Prodigal, it is not because he would be an idler, or the associate of idlers : *that* I had already pardoned ; but because he has dared to marry [*fiercely.*], and, do you hear, in the very face of my express prohibition.

Staun. [*astonished.*] Married ?

Stock. Yes, a beggar. Don't ask me more now ; you shall hear all — all to-morrow. I am too much worried now — you will forgive this inhospitality. To-morrow, remember, you have promised to make your home here.

Staun. [*Going.*] Well, good night, Stockton. Married!
[*musing.*] — 't is strange! A beggar? [*to himself, while moving to the door.*

Stock. Yes, [*ringing the bell for the porter to attend on Staun.*]
a beggar — a pitiful schoolmistress. [*opening the door.*

Staun. [*eagerly.*] Do you say so? My God! if —— Good
night, good night! [*Exit, precipitately.*

Stock. [*Looking after him with surprise, then closing the door.*]
Why he is mad too! There must be something in the moon.
[*Takes up the keys from the table.*] I imagine if Staunton's
cash were not safe under these keys [*putting the smaller ones
into his pocket.*], and these to boot [*hanging the large ones up,
in a closet.*] he would not be so generous with his lost heiress.
[*Rings a silver handbell.* — *Enter Peter at the door.*] Why
do you come? Where is Hans? Send him here.

Peter. He has this very instant, sir, gone out with a parcel,
for Miss Stockton.

Stock. That will do. [*Exit Peter.*] I'll be bound, to that
ungrateful —— Hans is mad too, I forgot that. My house
is nothing but a Bedlam, since —— O Arthur! Arthur!
[*sinking down in a chair, with his head in his hands.* — *Scene
closes.*

Scene II.

The Street, as in Act II. Sc. I.
The bookseller's shop is closed, but there is a
brilliant light in the window of a shop on the opposite
side, near the front of the scene.

Enter slowly, Staunton.
He moves towards the door of " No. 92 " — hesitates — then
turns back to the forepart of the stage.

Staun. There is surely a magic about this house, or I am
a bolder castle-builder at five and forty than while I was
young. My head is quite bewildered. Let me see what
grounds have I to be so fanciful, except the maddest of hopes.
That song! Why hundreds may sing it. Yet it was strange
too. Then the likeness in the fair author, a something that
struck at first, but was lost as I looked at her nearer; and
she was a schoolmistress, it appeared probable. Why should
she not be this young Stockton's wife? — And then if ——
God help me! the thought will make me crazy: I must — I
must get somehow into that house. Who is this? —

Enter Hans,
bearing a cabinet-picture covered over with a white cloth. He
touches his hat, and is about to pass Staunton,
who arrests him.

Why Hans, is this you? We shall have to be better acquainted, my good friend, now that I 'm to trouble your master for a day or two. [*Hans bows.*] What have you there?

Hans. A picture, Mr. Artur's — must go to him directly. [*going.*

Staun. [*stopping him.*] Mr. Arthur's? What! of him?

Hans. O no, sir, of hish vife.

Staun. [*eagerly.*] His wife? Quick! I must see it. [*Seizing it, begins to unpin the cover.*

Hans. Mein Herr, was wollen Sie? [55] Pardon me, but, — sir — Mr. Shtaunton! —

Staun. [*who has drawn the picture from the cover and contemplated it, by the light of the shopwindow, with marked emotion.*] She! the very same! the fair authoress, but less pale and more cheerful. Now, if the rest of my conjecture prove but true! Here, thank you, my man. [*giving the picture, and with it a piece of money.*] And there, I have put you to some trouble.

Hans. Tausend Dank! much obleegdt. Can you findt your way home alone, Mr. Shtaunton? [*arranging the cover again on the picture.*

Staun. O yes: *der Weg dahin ist nicht weit,* as you would say, my honest fellow; and before I get half through the distance I expect to meet my man, who was to come for me. Good night.

Hans. Goodt night, sir. [*Exit, entering "92" after the usual delay at the door, which is opened to him, during the following soliloquy of Staun.'s.*

Staun. [*pulling out his watch, and going again to the shopwindow to look at it.*] It is but a minute or two after nine.

I will venture to call there on the strength of her manuscript. What a pity I left it yonder! [*looking toward the bookseller's.*] But if it is she, I can make good my excuse: and if it is my!—— Heavens! what excuse shall I need?— Jack Doughty shall take me a note to prepare the way. *Theresa!* [*with a tender, yet rapturous tone.*] — Heaven grant it! [*Exit up the perspective of the street.*

Enter, from 92,

BUZZ.

He appears to be a little gay.

Buzz. "Joho, trallala, &c." Devil, if I can get that fellow's song out of my head! wish I was on the lark with Stockton about it. But here comes some other Yankee.

Enter, from the left,

LEDGER.

Ledger — a little stupid — but better than none. How are you, *old hoss?* as you say here in America. Let's have a spree! Oysters and fire-punch — or champagne and billiards — whatever you like.

Ledg. Nothing. You must excuse me altogether to-night.

Buzz. A row then with the Charlies, or a lark with the girls, or a roll into one of your coalholes among the niggers? I like your niggers; they're the only wits, poets, and mimics you have in America. Come, [*dancing and singing, negro-fashion :*

" We'll dance all night till de broad daylight,
" And go hum wid de gals in de mornin'."

I 'm your man for anything, Ledge : I 've got the devil in me ; it can't be that poor half-bottle of claret I have just swigged at Stockton's ; but damme, I 'm up for something !

Ledg. And you may go down for something, if you don't take care.

Buzz. [*swaggering.*] I down ? *I ?* Did you never see me play Bobadil ? But how could you ? it was at little Kelley's Theatre. But, I say, Ledge, if you 'll come to some nice place — or, faith, to my rooms if you like — only there 's Mrs. Pickins might not like it so well — no matter, if you 'll come I 'll give you a touch of real amateur-acting. " By Pharaoh's foot ! " [*imitating Bobadil.*] I 'll do it ! — Come, don't be ill-natured ; you shall play Cob.

Ledg. Thank you ; somebody else must grace your cudgel. It 's past nine ; and you know what work I have ahead.

Enter, from 92,

HANS, *and passes rapidly.*

Ah, Hans ! after the keys ? But you must hurry. Stay, — what if your master be in his room ?

Hans. I must den efen tell all to Miss Clara, and get her to call him out.

Ledg. Do so, in Heaven's name. Quick. [*Exit Hans, running to the right.*] Good night, sir. [*to Buzz.*

Buzz. You won't then. Well, you 're a [*Exit Ledg., entering* 92.] d——d surly Yankee ; and " Body o' Cæsar ! [*after Bobadil.*] but that I scorn to let forth so mean a spirit, I 'd have stabbed him to the earth."

Enter DOUGHTY,

who comes in contact with his stick, as he flourishes it,
and knocks it angrily aside.

Dy. The devil you would! You 'll have to aim lower then,
with your handspike.

Buzz. [*still as Bobadil.*] "Do you prate? Do you murmur?" [*offering to beat him, as Bobadil would Cob.*

Dy. [*knocking the stick out of his hand.*] Prate, and murmur?
Why what craft are you, that are so saucy with your hail?
Yes, pick it up, my rover [*as Buzz takes up his stick.*], but hark
you, don't you be running aboard of me again with it, or we 'll
get foul in earnest, and if we do —

Buzz. Why what then, you Yankee skipper?

Dy. Not quite so good as that, — only a second-mate, my
little Capting. But if we do get foul, as I say, can you tell
me how much of your running-geer will be left? [*pointing
contemptuously to Buzz's long hair, extravagantly long and
numerous watchchains, trinkets, &c.*] or whether I don't bring
down all by the board and make a mere wreck of you?

Buzz. Do you know whom you are talking to, you saucy
pirate?

Dy. Soft words, soft words, my land rat! we have steel
traps in this here country, we have, that 'll take such vermin
as you between the teeth in less than no time. Talking to?
I 'll tell you. I take you for one of those traveling Englishers
that come out of their own holes, because they are starved out
of 'em, or mayhap because a running-noose is not the kind of
granny's-knot they 're fondest of having tied in their cravats;

and so they come over here, where they meet with whole-souled
fellows, that ask no questions, but feed all the mouths that
open for them, and then, when their bellies are full, and they
get resty, they kick out their heels as if they were blood-
horses, and not old spavined jades after all, or vermin as afore-
said.   And what do you take me for, my poop-frigate that
would be, but cock-boat that are?

Buzz. [*Looking at him very superciliously, and drawling.*
Why, as you have that letter in your hand, you may be some
Yankee upstart's mongrel valet, half land-lubber — in your
own cant — and half-water-rat. —

Dy. Go on; take it easy. [*moving quietly a little nearer.*

Buzz. But as Yankees are too proud to be servants, or too
mean to have them, I take you for one of those barking curs
that never bite, one of those bragging —

Dy. Take it comfortable; don't hurry. [*getting a little nearer,
but still very quietly, and carelessly picking his teeth.*

Buzz. Bragging Jack-tars, that having seen a Yankee seventy-four sink an English gunboat, got vast notions of their
own powers, and began to think of —

Dy. Licking the British; and did it.   But don't you mistake the gunboat for a Chinese junk and the seventy-four for
your own steamfrigates?   I only ask for information: go on;
I'm in no manner of haste, and am fond of news.   [*still nearer,
and still quietly, but now stowing away in his pockets his tooth-
pick and the letter he carries.*

Buzz. In short, you insolent rascal, who dare thus to interrupt me, that have been dragged in a car by all your aldermen,
been *fêted* and *balled* till I was stunk to death by all your

ladies, that have paper-painted more rogues and fools in my own country than you ever are like to see in yours, and played Captain Bobadil to the delight of the most critical audience in the world, you, I say, are one of those broadside fighters that never come to close quarters when they can help it, and, when they do — "Tut!" [*Bobadilizing.*] "They have assaulted me some three, four, five, six of them together, as I have walked alone in divers skirts o' the town, where I have driven them before me the whole length of a street, in the open view of all our gallants, pitying to hurt them, believe me. Yet all this lenity will not overcome their spleen; they will be doing with the pismire, raising a hill a man may spurn abroad with his foot at pleasure. By myself I could have slain 'em all, but I delight not in murder."

Dy. [*using unconsciously the language of Young Kno'well in the same play.*] Are you so sure of your hand, then, Captain?

Buzz. [*entering into the spirit of his part.*] "Tut! never miss thrust, upon my reputation with you."

Dy. There then, [*twisting his stick from him and beating him.*] and there. Is that "close quarters"? — or would you have it closer? [*raising the stick again.*

Buzz. [*in the very attitude of Bobadil.*] "Hold, hold! under thy favor, forbear!"

Dy. That's the first word of sense you have spoke to-night. Yet, but that I am a valet as you say, to a better Englisher than yourself, I would make you talk more. [*flinging his stick to him.*] But I must do Mr. Staunton's bidding. [*Ringing at 92.*

Buzz. [*getting up.*] Staunton! The devil! Like master,

like man : that 's the rebel Englishman I met to-day, that thinks as well of these pigfeeding Yankees as if they were real men. 'Faith! they have some muscle too. [*rubbing himself.*] Heaven send he don't tell him! But if he do, he can't say I did n't play my part to the life. I must make a note of this. [*Goes to the window and writes.*] "Met a Yankee, and after drubbing him soundly, suffered him in turn to beat me a little, in order to practice Bobadil, which I really flatter myself I did to the life." There. [*shuts up his book, and Exit as*

92 lets in Dy.

Drop falls.

Act the Fifth

Scene I.   *The parlor of " 92 " — as in Act III. Sc. I.*

The pianoforte is seen open,
showing the keyboard and the maker's name in
front.   On the top of the instrument,
leaning against the wall, is a cabinet picture.
Theresa,
seated at the little writing-table, on which
is lying an open note.

Ther. Oh I it will be charming to add my little earnings to Arthur's, now too that he has lost all for my sake. [56] How fortunate I was I — and how fortunate that Arthur should be out now! for he must not know of my industry ; not yet at least. Yet [*musing.*] it is strange too ; how should this gentleman have found me out ? I must read this again. — "Make arrangements for future publications " —   That is well I and it almost turns my little head with delight. But why this haste ? · And — let me see : "Something assures me that on other accounts our interview may be of moment to both of us, as it certainly must be, in any event, of benefit to yourself and Mr. Stockton, of whose father I may boast to be an old friend." This seems to promise much indeed ! —   Yet there

is no name. — It will be well, at all events, to call in old
Martha. [*She moves to the door, when it opens and*

Enter STAUNTON.

*He comes forward, at first
with precipitation, then checks himself and bows.*

Staun. I should apologize for this sudden and abrupt visit —
but — I — I feel —

Ther. [*startled and embarrassed.*] Sir! Be seated. — You
seem —— Excuse me a moment; I but go to call my
woman.

Staun. [*hastily.*] No, no; do not. In fact, the immediate
motive to my calling was that I had seen a picture, in which
recognizing the lady I had the pleasure to encounter at the
stationer's, I could not doubt that Mrs. Arthur Stockton and
yourself were one.

Ther. Yes sir, it is a picture much treasured by my husband,
who took it when I was but fifteen, and on a visit to my
friend, his sister. [*She turns her head and looks toward the
picture. Staun. follows the motion with his eyes, starts, and moves
suddenly to the pianoforte.*

Staun. Good God! [*Turns round, with a look so earnest and
tender, to Theresa, that she trembles.*

Ther. Why, what is the matter, sir? Martha! [*calling, but
in a timid and agitated voice.*

Staun. Do not be frightened: I —— Tell me, was it you
I heard at twilight, this evening, singing an air of Lodoiska?

Ther. [*surprised.*] Sir! Yes — a simple song, that has no
attraction but that it was a favorite of my mother's.

Staun. [*more and more moved.*] My God! And that mother! was that — that her instrument?

Ther. [*partaking his agitation, but mingled with astonishment and some terror.*] Yes sir, — valued by her as being the gift of her mother to her when a child. We brought it with us from England, I have been told.

Staun. [*Supporting himself by a chair.*] Only one word more! Did that mother — bear the name of Staunton?

Ther. No, her name was Ellison. Yet, "Staunton" is familiar to me too. [*thoughtfully.*

Staun. How? Speak! — This is an awful moment.

Ther. There was a packet addressed to a Mr. Staunton of London, which, at her death, was found in her writing-desk, and forwarded —

Staun. To me! My child! my child! [*throwing his arms about Ther., and sobbing.*

Ther. [*extricating herself.*] Sir! I ——

Staun. Oh Theresa! —

Ther. Yes, that is my name. Are you — are you —— O my God, speak, sir!

Staun. I am — your father, Charles Staunton. That song was Catharine's, that instrument was hers, you are her likeness, and Theresa was my child. [*embracing her again. Theresa sobs.*] Yes, my daughter, weep; but weep for joy; or weep that your poor mother is not here to share our transport.

Ther. O sir, my father — for I cannot doubt that you are so — why have we been parted? why do we meet now?

Staun. Did then your mother never speak of me?

Ther. Never; and all my questions, when a child, were
10*

silenced severely. It was only when I was sixteen, a year before my mother died, that she showed me a sealed letter which she said was to be kept for my father, should he seek me out; but if I should attain my twentieth year, and hear nothing of him, I was then to open it.

Staun. O my poor child! that was your mother's self. But where, where is this letter? [*Ther. opens the writing-desk and takes out a letter sealed in black, which she first kisses, then hands to Staun.*

Staun. [57] [*reading the superscription.*] "To be delivered, after my death, to Theresa's father, when he shall voluntarily seek her; but if she attain her twentieth year unacknowledged by him, she is then to open this letter. She will there read her father's name, and know why she is left without a father's protection." O my Theresa! my daughter! you shall know that too from my lips. Let us break this seal. [*He pauses in the act, appearing to be overcome.*] I cannot do it: it seems to break my heart. Theresa, do you — But no, no! [*with an effort.*] it is fit that I should, and I only. [*Presses the seal to his lips, opens the envelope, and takes from it the letter, likewise sealed.*] See there, my child: "To Charles Staunton, Esquire," and, beneath the device, "C. S." Those are the initials of my wife, and your mother.

Ther. [*throwing herself into Staunton's arms, and kissing him fervently on the brow.*] O yes, you are indeed my father! My father, bless me, bless your child!

Staun. O Theresa, God in Heaven bless you! bless you for that I find you all a father could desire, — God Almighty bless you, my darling, my fair and virtuous child! — But this letter, *Theresa* [*dwelling on her name with great tenderness of accent.*] — I cannot read it to-night.

Ther. Do not, father; leave it till to-morrow: it would be too much for both now.

Staun. Yes, too much, at least for me. For even I shall have to ask your forgiveness, Theresa, — even your father ask it of his child.

Ther. No, no, do not talk so. Were you not benevolent to me, ere you knew me, — my friend, before my father? It was the will of Heaven if we have not met, and not your fault, my father.

Staun. Dear girl! Let me look at you. [*She kneels at his feet. He smooths her hair caressingly from before her forehead, looks on her for a long minute with deep emotion and admiration, then kisses passionately her forehead, and she sinks her head on his lap.*] My beautiful! — my child! my child! God bless you! [*Theresa sobs. — After a moment, gently raising her head, Staun. says:*] And now let us at once to your husband's father — to your friend's — to my friend's. O Theresa! there will be more joyful hearts than one at this discovery. [*He throws up the window, and, leaning out, calls.*] Jack! Jack Doughty!

Ther. And Arthur, father? my —

Staun. Your husband? Noble fellow! the man of all others to whom, had I the choice of thousands, I would have given you, my girl. [*Ther. throws her arms about him, and with her head on his breast, hugs him in silence.*

Enter DOUGHTY.

Come in, Jack; this is my daughter, — my new-found, long-lost child. He cannot speak for surprise. Theresa love, this faithful man has been more your father's companion than his servant; welcome him for my sake.

Dy. [*who has been throwing his eyes about the room, and now fixes them on the pianoforte.*] Perhaps, sir, Miss Staunton may welcome me for my own sake. Will she tell me, is she English-born?

Staun. [*smiling.*] O yes, of the true Bull breed, Jack.

Ther. I came over with my mother when I was but five years old.

Dy. And did she bring with her that fortepianner?

Ther. O yes: but why?

Dy. And was her name — let me see — Ellis ——

Ther. Ellison, we were called.

Dy. Hurrah! [*throwing up his hat and catching it.*] Forgive me, sir — forgive me, Miss Staunton; but I am happy too. Your father saved my life, and I saved his daughter's.

Staun. What is this? Speak!

Dy. Why sir, in the first place, you see, I knowed that pianner the moment I saw it, because it was hoisted out of hatches and opened for the customhouse lubbers to look at, to see if it was really an old one, and I remember the name, " George Astor, Wych Street, St. Clement's, London," on the plate there. Perhaps though, I might not have thought on 't again, but for what has turned up.

Staun. And the life? my child's? how was that?

Dy. O sir, we had a regular Sou'wester and shipped some heavy seas when the lady and her child came over. I was third mate of the packet, and was aft the next morning with my clasp-knife in my hand splicing an end of cable. The bulwarks to-starboard had all been stove-in the night before, and this little young lady, a child then, was looking out of the companionway-house door, it being fine weather then, but the sea rolling high after the storm, when the vessel gave a lurch, and the child, dashed against the house, was then pitched forward and capsized, and, but that I happened to be in the way, would have gone through the hole of the bulwarks. [*Staun. makes an exclamation of terror.*] I caught her, but we came on our beam-ends together, and in the fall the child ran foul of my knife, which made an awful gash in her little white arm.

Ther. [*shoving up her sleeve.*] See, father; see, my preserver, my friend; [*to Dy.*] here is the scar still. I am that little girl you saved for my father, as you say he saved you. [*she takes his hand a moment.*

Dy. [*brushing his hand over his eyes.*] Well — damn it! — Pardon —

Staun. No, Jack, this time, I *don't* hold my finger up.

Dy. Well sir, I was only going to say, that — O blas —! — I must swear — it, it is the happiest day of my life.

Staun. As mine was, my brave fellow, when, without knowing it, I gave in return a life for the one you had preserved, years before, for me. [*Dy. fairly sobs.*] Come now, [*pushing him out.*] go and call a coach; we must all be off on the instant to Mr. Stockton's. [*Exit Dy.*

Solemnly.] Now Theresa, while he is gone, let us pay our first thanks where we first owe them. [*The father and daughter take hands, and appear about to kneel, as the scene closes.*

Scene II.

The counting-room of Mr. Stockton.

All but complete darkness. ARTHUR *and* LEDGER *just discovered standing in the foreground.*

[58] *Arth.* How long do you think we have been here?

Ledg. I should say it was good ten minutes since Hans locked us in. But time passes slow, when one is waiting.

Arth. And waiting in the dark. It would hardly do to light a candle though: they would smell the match.

Ledg. Ten o'clock, was it not?

Arth. Yes, " at the stroke."

Ledg. And there it goes now. [*Clock in the room strikes the hour.*

Arth. And now to hide. [*beginning to grope about.*

Ledg. Take care: if we were to knock the screen down, it might be difficult to set it up again in this darkness.

Arth. Yes, in time. And there! hush! [*lowering his voice.*] the key is turning in the door now. Keep close. [*Deep silence, then*

Enter
SCHURK, *and two Burglars, preceded by* HANS.

Sch. Have you the matches?

Hans. Yes, here tey are on de mantlepiece, mit de candle. Don't shtir, any ones, or you 'll come foul of de screen. [*lights the candle, which reveals the scene.*

*A timepiece is seen on the mantlepiece ;
on the left of the fireplace, a huge iron safe ; on the right,
between a high desk and the fireplace, a frame
covered with green cloth, behind which are
ARTHUR and LEDGER.
Their feet and legs are hidden from the
other party by a long flat box, or countinghouse
foot-bench, and all the rest of their bodies by
the cloth of the screen.*

Sch. [*Kneels down before the safe, and applies to it a small chisel. The door opens.*] *Sieh da!* Mr. Stockton has the keys : much good may they do him ! It was as easy to make the bolts shoot back again, as to shoot forward. There is the specie : you 'll carry that. [*to the burglars, who nod.*] But first, for the books. [*Taking out the journals, legers, &c.*] Here, hold my cloak, Hans.

1st Burg. [*surlily.*] What 's all that for ?

Sch. That 's my business. But when I set the fire under them, may n't they burn with the house, and hide all, ha ?

2d Burg. *Wohlan*[5] ; but make haste : we 'm for de shiners, eh Bolton ?

1st Burg. When we get them, Dutchman. There 's your

firewood, and be damned. [*to Sch., flinging down a bundle of combustibles.*

> SCHURK *proceeds to pile the books over them and between*
> *them, opening the books and turning them*
> *inside down on the fuel.* HANS *suddenly throws the*
> *cloak over him, and wraps him in it, holding him down, and at*
> *the same instant the screen is thrown down, and*
> ARTHUR *and* LEDGER *spring forward over*
> *the box to the burglars.*

2d. Burg. *Wir sind verloren!* [making for the door.

> HANS *trips him, while the* 1st *Burglar*
> *fires a pistol at* ARTHUR. LEDGER *rushes between the*
> *weapon and his friend, and appears to receive the ball in his left*
> *arm, which drops by his side.* ARTHUR *knocks*
> *down the* 1st *Burglar, and after a brief*
> *struggle, both are overpowered.*

Arth. Ledger, bring a cord.   But you 're wounded!

Ledg. O nothing at all.   Will you hold both these scoundrels?

Arth. Yes. [*Ledg. goes up the scene.*] Hans, don't you stir : Schurk is armed and desperate.

Hans. I hafe him safe, Mr. Artur.   I remembers his threat fery vell.

Ledg. [*Returning with cords*].   These two we 'll commit to the watch.

Arth. But Schurk must with us.   [*Sch. groans.*

> *They begin to bind the prisoners, and Scene closes.*

SCENE III.

The parlor at Mr. Stockton's — as in Act I. Sc. I.

STOCKTON, MRS. STOCKTON, CLARA, STAUNTON, *and* THERESA, —
*the latter between Mrs. S. and Clara, who have
each one of her hands.*

Clara. My sister! [*putting her arm about Ther.'s waist, and
drawing her to her.*] What did I say to you, you dear one, not
an hour ago? Did I not tell you all would be well? You
see, even papa looks happy.

Staun. Yes, he's forgotten the beggar and schoolmistress,
eh Stockton?

Stock. Surely, for I see but the acknowledged daughter of
my friend. —

Staun. And his heiress. But forgive me this fling, Stockton. [*taking his hand.*] It were strange indeed, since your life
has been wholly commercial, if you did not set more value on
wealth than it is worth.

Stock. But only its due value on good name. You will
remember, Theresa's birth was libeled by that villain, Schurk.

Mrs. S. And it is hard to find one's children disappointing
all one's hopes.

Staun. And oh, such happiness when they fulfil them! [*clasp-*

ing Ther.'s hand in both his.] as even Arthur shall now be found to have done. [*turning to Stock.*

Enter Buzz.

Stock. Yes, but where is my boy? [*to Staun.*

Buzz. That is what I have come to tell you. But eh! this is an unexpected pleasure: you here, Mrs. Stockton? [*to Ther.*]. And you all look so happy! [*inquiringly to Stock.*

Staun. For the *Vice* is now one with *Virtue.*

Stock. And the fatted calf is ready for the *Prodigal's* return. Where is my son, sir? [*to Buzz.*

Buzz. I don't know what you mean by your calves and prodigals, nor have I been long enough in America to comprehend a virtuous vice; but I see there is something preparing for me to set down. As for your son, [*to Stock.*] he is about unmasking a villain; and the story was so good I could not rest until I had come to tell you.

Clara. It is Mr. Schurk, father; he has been plundering you, as far as I can understand, by false entries in the books —

Buzz. And to-night meditates burglary and arson.

Stock. Heavens!
Staun. What's this? } [*together.*

Buzz. [*declaiming.*] "Not wine — nor beer — nor brandy; it is vice — dishonor — death!"

Stock. What do you mean? Are you —

Buzz. Drunk? O no. But 'faith! Stockton, I never saw a better villain in my life. We heard it all, Arthur and I. —

Stock. And Arthur has gone ? —

Buzz. With Ledger to surprise him. [*Staun. rings the bell.*] Old Hans was to let the thieves in, with the keys, where they 'll find more than they look for. Is n't it great ? And you should have heard him sing, in his wish to do the gay thing and stire the devil out of countenance. " Joho, trallala, &c." [*singing as Schurk.*

Stock. Since you are so gay, my dear Mr. Pickins, do you go out and meet my son and his friend wherever you can, and bring them here.

Enter PETER.

Buzz. "By the foot of Pharaoh ! " I 'll do it. "Not wine " —— Rare villain ! [*Going.*

Staun. Permit me, Stockton. [*To Peter.*] Be so good as to send my man up here.

Peter. Yes, sir. [*Exit Peter.*

Stock. But stay, Pickins. Not a word to the young men of what awaits them.

Enter DOUGHTY.

Buzz. O no ! especially as I don't know what it is. Eh, the devil ! [*encountering Dy. on his way out.*

Dy. [*to Buzz.*] " Hold, hold ! under thy favor, forbear ! " — Pardon me, ladies and gentlemen ; but ——

Buzz. [*trying to slip money into his hand.*] It 's a rehearsal we had together to-night : " Every man in his Humor ". And I played it to the life ; did n't I ? [*winking to Dy. and endeavoring to force the money on him.*

Dy. Faith, you did; but I 'm not the doorkeeper: I take no fees but from my master.

Buzz. I must note that down too. [*Lugging out his mem. book and writing.*] There: "The Americans never take money, as a gift; though they borrow it without scruple, and *repudiate* for the interest." [*Exit.*

Staun. Ha, ha, ha. It 's enough, Stockton, to drive you Yankees mad with vanity, to see the pains that is taken to traduce you, by men who find all Europe unworthy of a single lie. But —— Oh, Jack, my boy, go down to Mr. Arthur Stockton's house, No. 92, you know, and sée if you can find him there — or on the way. Send the whole party —

Stock. Thieves and all.

Staun. Yes, you 'll find thieves among them — directly hither. [*Exit Dy.*

Stock. You will hardly believe it, when I tell you that that man, Pickins, has been more honored among us than anybody since Washington; and you see the result!

Staun. Which is exactly what I should have foretold. You neglect your own authors — I 've been but a few hours among you, Stockton, yet I 've visited a bookseller's already — have I not, my child? [*smiling significantly to Ther.*

Ther. Ah, father, do not betray me.

Staun. Not yet; we will wait for your lord and master. — Well, I 've heard enough, Stockton, to convince me that, great, and, I have no doubt, from the very malignity with which you are slandered, *good* people as you are, you still fall into the dangerous error of driving to the woods your own prophets and honoring wisdom and song only in those of other countries.

Stock. And they that turn their own children adrift, how shall they expect that strangers will not despise their professions of interest and affection? *I* have just escaped being taught that lesson, Staunton; but I see my countrymen learning it at large. They have taken the bread from the mouths of their own offspring, and flung it unto dogs.

Staun. That fawn awhile, but, on the first occasion, turn and rend them. It is Heaven's own equity. See here!

Enter

ARTHUR, — LEDGER (*his arm in a sling*), —
HANS (*with the keys of the countinghouse*) *leading* SCHURK,
whose head is sunk on his breast, — BUZZ (*who
stops short, and makes a note in his book,
looking the while at Schurk,*) —
and DOUGHTY.

Stock. My son! Arthur! [*clasping his hands in his.*
Arth. Father!

Stock. Will you forgive me?

Arth. O my father, it is I that need to ask that.

Stock. Well, we both have sinned. And you were watching over my interests, Arthur, the same day that I had seemed to separate you for ever from them?

Arth. I have done but my duty, sir. But there is Ledger: to him you owe it, that you have a son at all. He rushed between me and the pistol of one of the robbers, and received the ball in his arm that must otherwise have pierced my heart.

Stock. Mr. Ledger — Henry — come here. Clara — my daughter. [*He takes a hand of each.*] You that have saved the life of the brother may well be set over the happiness of the sister; you, that have shown ever such zeal for the interests of a master, will not be the less careful of them, for sharing them; nor have I forgotten your spirit, and your honor, sir, in the interview we had this evening. My son now, and my partner; let that be the reward of your virtue. [*Schurk strikes his hands heavily together.*

Clara. [*turning at the sound, and looking with compassion on Sch.*] And O my father, let it too be the sole punishment for that unhappy man.

Ledg. O sir, pardon him; for *my* sake, if I may ask it.

Stock. I will for his and my own; for the iron has entered his very soul. My son, [*to Arth.*] you do not speak.

Staun. I can explain his silence. He pities, with me, the criminal; but the law must pronounce upon the crime. Stockton, justice is above generosity; in its dispensation we imitate the gods: this man must go to prison.

Arth. [*mournfully, but firmly.*] It is but too true; or you do a violence to those arrested with him.

Stock. You are both right. Clara, do not speak for him. [*gently repelling her, as she presses up to intercede.*] Let me but ask him, what impelled him to this fatal act? [*Sch folds his arms, and looks inflexible, his head still bent down.*

Buzz. I will tell you. "Not wine — nor beer — nor brandy; it was vice — dishonor — death!"

Sch. [*starting.*] Ah! Traitor! [*to Hans.*

Stock. [*severely.*] No, sir; he who could write that letter was the traitor; he who could tempt a poor servant, as I suppose you did this faithful fellow [*looking at Hans.*] ——

Hans. If Mr. Shtockton vill permit me to spreak, I vould say dat to tempt me because for I vas his countryman vas vorse dan all. If my faterlandt send out some badt men, she sendt out many goodt men too, and to bring such a shtain on all honest Germans deserves in deir adopted country double punishment.

Staun. It is well spoken.

Buzz. I must note that. [*Writing.*] "I met but one American that had true pride of country, and he was a Dutchman."

Stock. Yet once more, let me ask you, Schurk, whether my kindness, my unbounded trust, deserved not better at your hands.

Sch. Ask nothing [*fiercely.*]; or put your question to the dicebox. Let me go.

Buzz. Yes, "Cards and dice, [*declaiming after Sch. in Act. iii. Sc. 3.*] if not the girls, have been too much for him. He 'll dice no more."

Arth. For shame, Pickins! Hans, lead the unhappy man to the carriage — Peter will aid you — and place him with the others; but do not be rough to him. [*Exit Hans with Sch.*] And now, father, explain to me: what is all this scene? why is Theresa here?

Staun. Because, sir, her father brought her hither. Yes, my son, in protecting Mr. Staunton's dollars, you have but secured what Theresa brings you towards an outfit in housekeeping. Arthur — let me call you so — [*taking his hand and that of Ther.*] I have found ——

Buzz. What, my friend of an hour, is that your daughter? And have you never seen her, till now, since you shot Frank Marston?

Staun. [*severely.*] Sir, sir! How can you allude to that unfortunate affair, at such a moment!

Buzz. Because perhaps I can do you a service you little look for. I have a letter — here, for aught I know, but at any rate in London — from Frank himself, written when he thought he was on his deathbed, showing most conclusively what a fool you were to suspect him, inasmuch ——

Staun. [*grasping his arm.*] And did he recover?

Buzz. Recover? — You hurt! [*rubbing his arm.*] — To be sure he did. Then you have n't seen in "Punch" the verses he addressed to me, scarce a month ago, from the Lake of Como, declaring me [*declaiming.*

> " Unstain'd by avarice, from all malice free,
> Truth loving for truth's sake, ordain'd to be
> New England's "—

Arth. [*to Ledg.*] Jest —

Buzz.   " New England's love, the Old's "—

Arth. Humbuggery.

Buzz. No, "idolatry." Eh! old book-pirate, what now? [*as*

Enter PROOFSHEET, *impetuously.*

Proof. [*in a voice of transport.*] Come along, Mr. Stockton! [*to Arth.*] — Ah! [*looking round with amazement.*] I beg pardon.

Arth. But what is the matter? Has my play failed?

Proof. Failed ? Triumphant! The curtain has dropped amidst such roars of applause as I never heard before —

Buzz. Ah! you should have heard my Bobadil!

Proof. — And I have come to carry the author before the audience, who are yelling for him as if mad.

Arth. It is well; but I have a happier drama here.

Proof. But sir, Burton [60] can scarce keep the house quiet.

Arth. Then he must let it rock. I have won more here to-night than ever a theatre can give me. Look around.

Staun. Ah sir, [*to Proof.*] I see you recognize the pretty authoress.

Arth. What ?

Ther. Forgive me, Arthur.

Staun. For what, you silly one ? For doing good, as he has done ? You shall know all about this, by and by, Arthur, with other matters. You, Mr. Proofsheet, shall still publish the "Schoolmistress", and at the "Mæcenas"'s expense. This, sir, is my daughter, your neighbor of "92", and your pet author's wife.

Stock. [*to Proof.*] Come, sir, as you have added to our joy as well as witnessed it, you must make one with us to-night at an impromptu supper —

Staun. Where I will unfold the whole plot of our domestic drama.

Stock. Which, Arthur, you shall, when you will, reduce to writing, and we will make a present of it to Burton for his theatres. But Pickins, what are you doing there ? [*to Buzz, who has drawn his eternal memorandum-book from his pocket, and commenced writing.*

Buzz. I am setting down the fact, that in America a man may at last write, even for the Stage, without being despised as for a mean action, and made to starve as for a silly one.

Staun. [*aside to Stock.*] The first genuine bill in his whole pocketbook of *Notes.*

Curtain falls.

NOTES

NOTES TO THE PRODIGAL

1.—P. 121. THE PRODIGAL; OR A VICE AND VIRTUE.] This title may be considered unsuitable, as *Arthur* is not a Prodigal except in his father's eyes, and that by a passionate malevolence and the rancor of disappointed ambition, which convert in a moment what was once to him a Virtue into a positive Vice. Any of the following names may be substituted, or a combination of any two of them, for the present title, which I retain, myself, only because of the allusions to it here and there in the play : —

1. *The Wilful Heir ; or Money and the Muses* [*or, A Vice and Virtue.*]
2. *Money and the Muses.*
3. *Wit and Wealth; or The two Merchants.*
4. *The Lost and the Found; or the India Merchants.*
5. *The Poet and the Merchant.*
6. *Plot and Counterplot.*
7. *The Merchant and the Merchant Mæcenas.*

2.—P. 121. — *Stockton!*] Omit, after this, to "do not swear!" then, in the same paragraph, all between "first-born" and "whom you called"

3.—P. 12?.   — *a father that* —]   Omit the rest of the sentence : then, in the next, all between "feel this fear" and "what then does."

4.—P. 124.   — *reminded*]   Omit from here to " But for this."

5.—P. 124.   — *Ellison* —]   Omit from this name to "come over"; also the words, "husbandless, all but pennyless: " then the sentence commencing "She had."

6. — P. 125.   — *a brute :*].   After this omit to "or did I," 8th line below, reading it "But did I, etc."

7.—P. 125.   — *You know that* —]   Omit to "conscience" (inclusive.)   Then recite the rest of the part thus: "I not only did that, but, when afterward their friendship had grown to love, did I not gravely take him to task as a father should? What did he reply? what, this dutiful, this good son, your poet, *etc.*"

8.—P. 126.   — *memory* —]   Omit from here to —"lest."

9.— P. 127.   — *day* —]   And from here to "I cast him off."

10.— P. 128.   Mrs. S. *Ah, my dear,* etc.]   Omit this and the next paragraph.

11.—P. 129.   — smashed —]   The rest of the stage-direction to be disregarded.

12.—P. 129.   — much —]   Omit from here to "one." By *Fish,* Hans means "Fesch" (as I remember the name) whose collection in Rome was sold in '44, and was much talked of at the time. Further on in the part, p. 130, omit from "at me" to "I take"; which read "So I takes."

13.—P. 130. — *comes here.*] After this, omit to "But dere's de bell," 13th line below.

14.—P. 130. — *sent him.*] Omit the rest of the paragraph.

15.—P. 132. Schurk.] His German accent is to be but slightly marked, the chief peculiarity of his English being, as is usual with foreigners, a more deliberate enunciation of the unemphatic syllables, whereby a word gets sometimes a twofold accent. For example, *Stock'ton* will be pronounced *Stock'ton'*.

16.—P. 133. — das ist ärgerlich.] *That is vexatious :* which may be substituted if preferred ; for, although Schurk makes the reflection to himself, as if impulsively, he is conscious that Stockton hears and understands him, and he means that he shall. So, presently, "Ach, ja!" — *Ah, yes!* and —"in der That! &c." — *indeed, I believe you!* The German is retained in the text, because it is absolutely more natural, as Schurk affects to speak from impulse and in a quasi-abstraction.

17.—P. 134. — *right ?*] Omit the rest of the part.

18.—P 134. — *wickedness* —] Omit from here to the semi-colon.

19.—P. 134. — *bound* —] Omit from here to " how ": then the interrogation, "Has he not had, etc.": then, all after the next interrogation to the one commencing " had I any reason " —: then from " disappointment " (inclusive) to " I should have felt."

20.—P. 136. — *not.*] Omit from this period to — " he is like " —: then the whole of the sentence commencing, "It has been."

21.—P. 138. — *secret ?*] After this, omit to "But I must" —
substituting a brief pause, as of thought.

22.—P. 139. Welch ein Glück !] *How lucky !*

23.—P. 141. Ey, Hans, &c.] *Eh, Hans, dear ! — What ails
you ?*

24.—P. 141. Wohlan !] *Well ! —* "Frisch ! " *Brisk !*

25.—P. 142. — *and yet,* —] Omit from this comma to the
next; and then, the clause commencing with "though" and end-
ing with "Philadelphia."

26.—P. 144. — *third place* —] Omit the clause between the
two dashes, and after this between the two semicolons.

27.—P. 146. — *at the Chestnut.*] This name will vary with the
locality of the representation ; or the three words may be omitted. —
The same remark (as to change of name) applies to the Scene itself
of the play, which (*mutatis mutandis*) may be New York, or Bos-
ton, or any other large commercial city of the Union.

28.—P. 148. SCENE II.] This Scene may be entirely omitted, or
largely exscinded : for ex., from the stage-direction, *Proof. again
bows,* p. 148, to the words, — "tell me however," on p. 152, reading,
in the part where these occur, "young Stockton" for "this young
gentleman" ; and again, on p. 153, all from " *Staun.* Certainly " —
to " *Staun.* One moment."

29.—P. 157. SCENE IV.] This Scene too to be omitted, or
greatly abridged.

30.—P. 164. SCENE I.] This also may be thrown out, at the

discretion of the manager. If admitted, it will be with the excisions indicated below, — 31-37.

31.—P. 165. — *Peter* —] Omit to the period. Then the word "expressly", and the clause from "papa" to the semicolon.

32.—P. 167. *O never*, etc.] Omit this first sentence.

33.—P. 168. Ledg.] Read the part: "Circumstances obliged me to, *etc.*"

34.—P. 168. Ledg.] Omit all to — "to-day there arrived" — p. 169.

35.—P. 169. *However* —] Omit the rest of the sentence. Then, from "They" to "character" (inclusive).

36.—P. 170. — *head.*] After this, omit to "I am ready" — 8th line below.

37.—P. 170. Ledg.] Omit the first sentence.

38.—P. 174. — *wholesome.*] From this, omit to "But — Ah! here is" — 14th line below.

39.—P. 179. — *nature* —] After this, omit to "I must now make" — 10th line on the next page.

40.—P. 180. — *to spare.*] Omit the rest of the part.

41.—P. 181. Bier? *&c.*] *Beer? No! no! brandy — wine-brandy!* Further on: "So sei es" — *Be it so:* "Tändelei!" *Nonsense!:* "Schon gut! schon gut!" *Well! well!:* "Dank!" *Thanks!*

42.—P. 183. — dass sie, *&c.*] — *destruction overtake her!* (lit.: *may the thunder and the storm strike her dead!*)

43.—P. 183. Aber wenn du dann ——] *But if thou then ——* "Sieh da !" *See there !*

44.—P. 184. "Was gleicht, *u. s. w.*"

> *On earth what is like to the hunter's enjoyment,*
> *To whom doth life's beaker give bubbles so bright?*
>   (or : To whom is the bead on life's wine-cup so bright ?)

45.—P. 185. "Kartenspiel, *u. s. w.*"] From Caspar's drinking-song, in the same opera : —

> *Play of cards and sport of dice,*
> *And a lass with bosom nice,*
> *Help to life that 's joyous !*

46—P. 185. Strafe mich Gott !] Literally, *God punish me !* But a rougher phrase would be the analogous one in English.

47.—P. 185. Herr Wirth !] *Landlord !* Below : " Ganz recht ! " *Quite right !* : — " mit dem Schlag " (*sc.* zehn Uhr.) — *at the stroke* (of ten.) : " Ganz gewiss, &c." *Most certainly. Come, come ! At,* etc. The English for this last phrase may be substituted : but it is not so natural, for the there and then.

48.—P. 186. — *the Duke of Wellington's* —] To-day : " Glad-stone's " (or " John Bright's.")

49.—P. 186. *I never played,* etc.]

" Miss Kelly's Theatre, Soho, London, was, on the morning of Saturday last, the scene of an unique performance, several of the leading dramatists and popular writers of the day having determined to give their friends a 'touch of their quality' as amateur actors. The play was Ben Jonson's 'Every Man in his Humor', with the following cast :

" *Kitely*...Mr. Foster : *Knowell*...Mr. Mayhew : *Captain Bobadil*...Mr. C —— D —— " : &c. &c.

" Foreign Miscellany ", in a New York paper of —— 1845.

50.—P. 188. — *breaking.*]   From this word, omit to "My father" —: then, throw out — " in the aristocratic order of things."

51.—P. 189.   — *a home* —]   From this, omit to the end of the sentence: then, after " at last," two sentences, to "Why need," on the next page.

52.—P 190.   *He was a man,* etc.]   Omit all the rest of the part, with the exception of the last simple sentence, reading there " he " for "Marston."

53.—P. 192.   Staun.]   Read the first sentence, simply, "I could never ascertain."

54.—P. 193.   *I should.* etc.]   Omit this clause: then, in the next sentence, from the semicolon to — " if she — "

55.—P. 196.   Mein Herr, *u. s. w.*]   *Sir! what would you?*   And below: " der Weg dahin ist nicht weit " — *it is not a great way off.*

56.—P. 203.   *How fortunate,* etc.]   Omit this sentence.

57.—P. 206.   Staun. [reading, &c]   Read the part thus : " *Staun.* [*after reading silently the superscription.*]   Let us break, *etc.*"

58.—P. 210.   Arth.]   Omit the three first paragraphs, and commence at " *Ledg.* Ten o'clock, &c."

59.—P. 211.   Wohlan —]   " Well " —   And below : " Wir sind verloren ! "   *We are lost!*

60.—P. 221.   *Burton* —]   Of course, for this name (both here and below) will be substituted some other, to suit the time and place of representation.   Or, read simply : " the manager."